CHRISTINA MERCER

ISBN: 978-0615776378

LIBRARY OF CONGRESS CATALOG IN PUBLICATION DATA 2013903702

Distributed in the U.S.A.

Christina Mercer
P.O. Box 1845
Shingle Springs, CA 95682

www.christinamercer.com

Hosted by indie-visible ink
www.indie-visible.com

Cover art by Chelsea Starling
Formatted by Novel Ninjutsu
Edited by Susanna Rosen

Dedication

For Dwayne and our boys,
Joshua and Quinton.

And for Grandpa,
who inspired me to achieve my dreams.
You will always be remembered.

Contents

With misty breath, the magic spins
Like webs within my soul;
Enchanted blood, forever kin
To my master's cruel hold.

— Grandma's Grimoire

Roots

Nettles stung Lia's flesh. She pressed her fingers against her mouth for relief. *This is what I get for letting my thoughts wander.* Grandma wouldn't have been so careless while harvesting sting-leaf. She wouldn't have let the villagers' opinions prick at her mind, no matter how many called her mad for crafting remedies in the old ways.

Koun whined and nudged Lia's arm with his nose.

"I'm all right, boy." Lia gazed into her hound's violet eyes and then turned her attention to the friendlier mallow plant. Its white flowers matched Koun's coat and its leaves and roots promised a soothing balm for the nettle's bite. She'd make another batch of salve for Da, too. He swore her "potions" kept his hands fit enough for hewing wood and soft enough for holding Ma. Her ma could use a bit more mallow infusion for her soaps, as well, and she'd take a bundle of clippings to Granda—

Her thoughts scattered as Koun shot from the garden. Lia whirled around to the pair of horses charging up the path. She squinted in the dusky light and recognized Da's friend, Kenneth, on one of the horses. Then her insides went cold. Across the other horse's back lay Da's limp body.

She dropped the harvested mallow and sped from her garden toward them. Ma's scream shot like a bolt through her, but Kenneth's words, "He's alive," offered Lia a morsel of hope.

Kenneth carried Da into the cottage, and Lia caught a glimpse of her father's torn and bloodied clothing. "I'll fetch Granda," she cried, and hurried to her filly.

Clad in her usual boy's breeches and high leather boots, Lia raced her horse down the path with her heart pounding in rhythm to the hoof beats.

Stay strong, Da! Just a little longer, and Granda will be there to heal you.

Why hadn't her dreams forewarned her? What good were fate-dreams if they showed when the mares would give birth or when visitors were coming from afar, but failed to give a timely warning for Da?

She blazed across waves of shamrock green hills dotted with the ancient quartz towers unique to Rockberg. She turned down the main road and rushed into the heart of the village. A few villagers lifted curious eyes, but many only cast contemptuous looks her way.

Let them glare until their eyes fall from their hollows.

She jumped off her horse and bolted into the makeshift store where she found Granda Luis at the counter cutting willow-weed. "Come quick!"

Her grandfather's brow shot up and he reached for his walking staff. "What's happened, child?"

"Da went chopping in the Bryns. Kenneth brought him home," she stifled a sob, "passed out and covered in blood."

Granda headed for the door, and Lia hurried outside and untied his horse while he walked as fast as his ailing legs would allow. Granda pulled himself into the saddle, wincing. Just then, two women in lacey frocks passed, scowling at them. More newcomers from Nemetona's southlands, more people to shun the old ways.

Lia set her jaw tight and mounted her horse. She didn't give a thistle about what they thought. All that mattered now was Da. With a silent nod from Granda Luis, they urged their horses into a run and left a cloud of dust behind them.

They roared like a gust of wind from the marketplace to the outskirts of town. Granda gripped his amber-tipped staff like a fighting lance, and he offered no explanations to the villagers despite the cries of alarm his urgent pace claimed.

They turned off the road and darted around the towers of quartz, lofty prisms standing proud and brilliant in the setting sun, and sped down the path to the whitewashed cottage.

"Lia girl, grab m'satchel," Granda said, dismounting his horse.

Lia's heart stampeded as she unstrapped the travel bag full of concoctions while Granda hobbled ahead.

Koun greeted her as she entered the cottage, whining and nosing against her. "Easy, boy," she soothed. She ran a hand over his snowy fur and hurried to the bedchamber.

She neared Da's bed and halted. Her chest tightened and tears stung her eyes. Oozing green blisters dotted his body like a strange pox, and jagged red sores covered the spaces in between.

She'd never seen her beloved da hurt or sick beyond a winter fever before this day. He was always her rock, hammering away on a new table or bench in his woodshop, tilling soil for her gardens, or teaching her how to hunt with her bow. And whenever he accompanied her to town, his quick wit put anyone with a wagging tongue in his or her place.

Ma lifted his head and struggled to pour some ale between his lips. She placed a wet cloth on his forehead, and then turned to Granda Luis. "Kenneth's gone ahead to fetch Doc Lloyd. Surely, between the two of you, something can be done."

Granda nodded, though storm clouds had settled on his brow.

Lia peered at Da's riddled flesh and a chill crawled up her spine. Her mind spun with recollections of the handful of elders that had come into Granda's store the past week, imploring him for a remedy to help their kinsmen. Like Da, the men were carried back from their hunting or chopping treks in the eastern Bryns, all feverish, pained and blighted by sores.

"His sores . . . the strange blisters . . . just like the others." Hope

4

withered like leaves within Lia. She and Granda had tried to craft skin salves and decoctions to cure the odd symptoms. Granda searched through Grandma's *Grimoire* for a remedy, but Lia knew every word of the beloved book, and nowhere on its pages did it mention such ills.

If Granda couldn't help the others, how could he heal Da?

The lump in Lia's throat grew thicker. Her family was everything. She had no friends, save her hound Koun and the horses. She spent every waking hour in Granda's store, in her gardens, or in Da's woodshop. It was a simple life, and fine by her, but now it was starting to splinter.

Ma's lips trembled. Several strands of copper hair escaped from her bun, clinging to the sweat beading her face. "He felt fine this morning, eager to go chopping. What could have possibly happened?"

"Briars, roots . . . took hold," Da sputtered, "dragged me down . . . I held to Merrie's lead . . . she ripped me . . . from them." His muscles tensed, and his feet writhed under the quilted coverlet.

Roots? How can roots reach up or drag someone?

"It's all right. Rest now, Dylan. Just breathe easy, and rest," Ma cooed, gently stroking back tendrils of his ash-blond hair. "Kenneth said he found him passed out more than a hundred feet from the half-chopped tree, Merrie standing over him, her lead rope still clenched in his hands."

Lia shot a beseeching look at Granda Luis, but his eyes never left

Da.

"What sort of roots?" she barely uttered the words before Doctor Lloyd waddled into the room with his face flushed like a beet.

"'Tis something breaching the walls of the northlands, from Brume, young lassie," the doctor said in the thick tongue of the older generations. He mopped his brow with the sleeve of his tunic. "This morning, young Shawn watched black roots covered in barbs sharp as a hedgehog's reach through Brume's mists and grab hold of his uncle. If he hadna been there to hack it away, well, I don't think his uncle'd be in his bed this eve. Dylan here makes twelve now this week in Rockberg, and Doc Maddox in Kilnsgate sent word today of nine there, and he's heard of six over in Springdale. With the growing number of attacks, official warnings are going out to all the northern villages."

"It cannot be." Ma's face blanched. "Something's found a way through the fog of Brume?"

Lia's heart thundered in her chest. Brume—the forbidden land. The land that had captured her fascination with her first glimpse of the writings in Grandma's *Grimoire*. Brume was where Grandma and Granda used to venture in safety when all others perished in the fog. Certainly, Granda would know something of the monstrous roots, and maybe a way to defeat them.

"Aye, Carin," the doctor nodded at Ma, "'tis something aggressive and poisonous. The barbs inflict a strong bane, almost like snake venom, even though 'tis a kind of plant. None we've treated show any improvement; our curatives don't appear to work on this."

Lia clasped Ma's arm and they stepped aside. The doctor placed his hand on Dylan's forehead. Da struggled for every breath while thick fingers probed for a pulse.

"I'm so sorry, lad. We're all puzzling this out." The doctor retrieved a glass vial from his bag and handed it to Carin. "'Tis a sleeping draught. Just two drops, three times a day. Keep the cool cloths coming, and as much water as you can get down through those lips. I 'spect your father here has some remedies to use on these wounds."

Doctor Lloyd turned and peered over his spectacles at his old friend. "In fact, Luis, I'll be needing to pick up some more skin salves and whatever else you think'll help. You're still the only survivor I know of that forbidden place. Got any ideas 'bout what could be coming through Brume's fog?"

Lia pinned her eyes on Granda Luis. Hope sparked within her. Now that Granda knew where the attack roots came from, he'd surely be able to craft a cure for the poison. She pressed her lips together, waiting for him to answer Doc Lloyd, just as she'd waited her whole life to hear him speak of the mysteries in Brume.

Granda sat quietly on a stool with his walking staff gripped in his hands. He pulled his eyes from his ravaged son-in-law and fixed them on his old friend. "I'd wondered the cause o'such strange ailin's, hoping they didn't link to Brume. Been a lifetime since I've trekked there, Lloyd. Not since the royal guard came here banning any attempts to breach the borderlands. And by the time those fools went back to the southlands, m'stiff old legs had turned for the worse."

Granda's brow furrowed and they all waited for him to continue. "I never entered Brume through the eastern hills, only through the southern border at Dunley Meadow. But if there's truly a wild root breaking through, well, I can only venture to guess."

"Hmm," Doc Lloyd nodded, "well the warnings should keep most away from the Bryns." He grabbed his bag and patted Ma on the shoulder. "Stay strong for him, lass. I'll check back here tomorrow afternoon. Luis, Lia."

The doctor walked out, and Lia peered at Granda. "There must be something we can do."

"Aye, girl." Granda Luis dug out several pouches from his satchel. "I've a few blends might purge some of the poison and help ease the pain, but there's only one way to find a real cure."

Granda's ice-blue gaze shifted between Lia and Ma. "I'm going back in, back into Brume. I'll leave at first light."

"Then I'm going too," Lia blurted, her heart lifting with hopefulness.

"No!" Ma cried, her eyes brimming with fear. "Not that dreadful place. You cannot, I forbid you."

"I'll be careful, Ma," Lia countered. "You know I'll follow Granda's orders. He needs me there this time; his legs are weak and I can tend to them. I can set up camp, cook, hunt, and gather what we need for the cure."

Granda Luis did not interrupt. Instead, he grabbed his things.

"You've no idea the dangers you face." Ma's voice cracked. "It's too risky, and you're only—"

"Fifteen is a grown woman by all standards. Three villagers my age are already married. And I'm more capable outdoors than most." Determination settled like gritstone within Lia.

Years of sadness lined Ma's face. Lia knew Grandma Myrna had sequestered herself in the shrouded land of Brume, scrambling between two homes to keep the old crafts alive. Then her unexpected death came at the worst time for Lia's ma—a young bride that same year, with only a moon to go before giving birth to her first and only child.

"Well, fine then, just dig me a hole right now," Ma said, tears welling. "Because I'll not want to see another day once I lose you."

Lia's heart ached for her mother, but her resolve to help Da would not falter. "Ma, I know how you feel about that place, but I have to go. You heard Granda. The only way to save Da from the poison is by going to Brume to find the cure, and I need to be there to help Granda do that. Please, we all must do what we can."

Granda Luis paused by the door. He gave Lia his familiar nod of approval, and then shifted his eyes to Ma. "Such events force our hands in startling ways. There are risks to any journey, but I know the way through the fog, and unless much has changed in the southern region, I know what dwells on the other side of it. We'll not tarry in Brume. Give us four days, maybe five, to return with a proper cure.

9

And with any luck, we'll put an end to this vile blight." Then he turned and stepped outside.

Ma closed her eyes and squeezed Lia's hands. Tears streamed down her face, as she whispered, "Your granda means every word he says, has complete faith in his skills, but there's danger in Brume neither of you is safe from. I've never ventured there, nor do I know firsthand who or what dwells in such a place, but I do know the dread seeping from my bones."

Ma's eyes met Lia's, green to green. "Please, go only where you must, Lia, and make haste home. Your da would rather perish than have you harmed trying to help him."

Ma took a deep breath, hugged Lia, and followed Granda's footsteps out the door. Lia didn't harbor the same fear of Brume that Ma did. She'd be safe with Granda and they'd be home with special herbs or bark or whatever made up the cure before the week was out. She was sure of it. Then she could tell Ma all about Brume and put an end to her fears once and for all.

"I'm going to find a way to save you, Da, I promise." Lia reached for her father and kissed his brow, an inferno burning beneath her lips. He made a slight motion with his hand toward her, before it fell back onto the bed.

She grabbed her knapsack, always packed with a good supply of herbs, and slung her crossbow and a quiver full of bolts over her back. Ma stood waiting outside under a starlit sky, her eyes rimmed in red, and she trembled in Lia's arms as they embraced.

Ma sniffed, her tears never ceasing. "I have dreaded this moment since you were a little girl talking to insects and mashing flowers in your water mug. You're so like your grandma, Lia."

"Ma, I'm only going to Brume for Da, and to be there for Grand—"

"Of course you are. And then you'll come home straightaway." Her lips tugged into a hard smile, a thin crack upon fine porcelain. She ran her hand down the length of Lia's red tresses. "Be sure to plait your hair, and you must take my cloak. It's thicker."

Before Lia protested, Ma flew back into the cottage, breathlessly returning with her jade-green cloak, two loaves of rosemary bread, a full pouch of jerked venison, two of her handcrafted soap bars, and a boar bristle brush.

"Let me help you." Lia grabbed hold of the items, stuffing them into her saddlebags.

"Remember to keep warm and dry, wash your face and hair, and . . . try not to be so brave!"

Lia rode astride her young bay, Shae, alongside Granda and his chestnut mount, Dobbin. They ran the horses under a crisp night sky, her snow-white hound following close behind. She was raring to set off on their journey, but Granda quickly reminded her they had to prepare, and with no clear roads leading to Brume, it was best to travel by daylight. That meant seven more hours before they could leave.

Seven more hours without a cure.

She forced back the urge to argue with Granda. He knew best. He was in charge. And she resigned herself to the wretched waiting.

They cantered through the sleepy town and Lia glanced at the village notice board. There hung numerous royal decrees for all to see, the parchment torn and frayed with age. She didn't need to stop to read them. She knew them all by heart, had already broken several, and was about to break another:

> *His Majesty of Nemetona, our noble King Brennus, and his royal sages set forth that the uninhabited northern land known as Brume is a dangerous region of deadly sea crags and barren knife-edged mountains. Attempting to breach its unyielding mist is prohibited,as is its glorification by the spread of foolish and unfounded tales.Those found disobeying these laws are to be reported at once to the sheriff appointed to this bailiwick.*

"Barren land and foolish tales," Lia mumbled. "More like a barren king and foolish sages." They were nothing like the rulers of old who had named Nemetona in honor of the land's sacred groves. And they knew nothing of the mysteries in Brume.

No matter, she thought. She'd soon see for herself the plethora of herbs and trees thriving beyond the wall of fog. That much Granda Luis freely told her. However, she had to ponder the old tales for further answers, including the mysterious way her grandparents had ventured into the northland without vanishing like all the rest.

Words from Grandma's *Grimoire* echoed inside her head:

> *Fogged, bogged gates of Brume, barrier to my home;*
> *Timeless, faceless watchers loom, but I am allowed to roam.*

So many legends, mystical poems, and riddles she had

memorized from Grandma's book. It was the closest thing she had to knowing her wise elder. Lia often envisioned Grandma concocting potions, or imagined hearing her spin wondrous tales of the ancient world. Whenever some nasty villager spat an unkind remark, she fantasized Grandma Myrna was there, turning the ignorant dolt into a wiggling worm to work in their herber garden.

Lia had asked Granda Luis about many of the riddles, whether the tales were mere fables, and if dwarfs had truly existed in Rockberg. His reply: "Poetic mazes, my dear, veiled paths to the truth. Your grandma wrote them to guard her knowledge, offering a worthwhile quest to those who would know their meanings." Then he'd give her a wink, enticing her to the challenge.

One verse she found, however, had caused Granda's brow to furrow and his mood to turn pensive. The riddle had both fascinated and haunted Lia from the moment she had spotted it scrawled in tiny script on a sketch of a flowering meadow. It read:

> For the call of magic, I do what I must;
> Sacrifice is needed to do what is just.
> The dark master beckons, and his command I do heed;
> Anything I will do for flower, root, and seed.
> And after my life does perish,
> And the magic fades toward its end,
> I know the children will come forth and bring it back again.

They halted in front of Granda's store and Lia broke from her thoughts and dismounted Shae.

"Lia girl," Granda said, still mounted atop Dobbin. "Ready a measure o'salve and sleeping tea to leave for your father. Use the strong formula with the—"

"Vandal root," Lia finished.

Granda Luis nodded. "Pack the usual remedies for our journey. We'll gather bits along the way, and plenty while we're there, but it's best to be prepared."

Koun's red-tipped ears lifted and a low growl rumbled in his throat. Lia turned to the mumblings of a few villagers heading home from the tavern, either too wary or too drunk to ask questions. Rockberg drew more people by the day from the oppressive southlands, all leaving the heart of Nemetona's kingdom in search of cleaner air and more room. And with them, they brought a fear of the old crafts.

"I need a word with Bran next door," Granda Luis said, interrupting Lia's thoughts. He turned Dobbin and trotted him into the night.

"Come on, Koun." The dog blinked his violet eyes at Lia and followed her into the store. The shop sat adjacent to Granda Luis's cottage. From the outside, it looked nothing more than a barn. But on the inside, shelves lined the walls with bottles of curatives, bundles of herbs dangled from hooks on the ceiling, and against the far wall stretched an enormous wooden counter holding mortars and pestle stones, and the handbreadth-thick book known as Grandma's *Grimoire*.

"I've elf leaf and melissa," Lia said, prompting Koun to cock his head at her. "But we'll need bridewort for Granda's aches, knitbone and dragonwort for wounds, maythens for sleep, and featherfew for pain."

Lia found a measure of distraction working the herbs. Her task focused her thoughts on the best way she could help, and she loved crafting blends more than anything. Sweet or bitter, soft or spiny, woody roots with fleshy insides or leafy greens plump with oils, every plant she touched enlivened her deep within.

She packed already made tinctures and unguents, honeycomb she'd extracted that same day, and a supply of linen strips and nettle cloth. For Da, she prepared blends for sleep and pain, bagged a mix of plantain and gypsywort for poultices, and then pulled out their vat of salve. She scooped the goopy wound salve into a jar, which gave way to a sudden tickle at her chest.

She pulled at the leather thong around her neck, brought up the leather pouch, and released the quartz stone held snug within. Koun had found the crystal piece that same week. He had dropped it from his mouth while Lia worked in the garden, its longest point flashing bright against the hound's nose.

The quartz grew hot and she flinched, dropping it into the jar of salve. The concoction liquefied against its heat and Lia thought sure the quartz glowed. But when she dug it back out, it was cool and clear once again.

Is my mind playing tricks? Perhaps the heat's from handling that bundle of herby grass.

"I must be getting tired," she murmured to Koun, who eyed her through a tangle of fur. She wiped the crystal clean and slipped it back into its pouch, cinching it shut.

The moon slipped past midnight as she and Granda finished their tasks and settled in his small cottage. With a handful of hours still to wait, they sat down to pottage and crusty bread, and Lia forced the food down into her anxious stomach.

Koun whimpered at her feet, his rust-tipped ears twitching. She stroked his white coat and his eyelids grew heavy. At Granda's prompting, she shuffled to bed. Her nerves told her sleep was out of the question, but her head barely hit the pillow when slumber stole her away.

Thick, unrelenting fog swirls all around. A cold chill shivers down her spine as sinister laughter reverberates in the distance. She strains to see something, anything, through the blinding mists. What lurks out there? She barely notices the caress of tendrils moving up her legs, encircling and binding them. The horrid cackle grows louder, its source much closer now. No! Get away! Then something on her breast burns, searing into her flesh. She cries out, but no sound comes forth . . .

Buds

*L*ia awoke clawing at her blanket. Her eyes darted around Granda's spare bedchamber and she let out a sigh of relief. *Just a nightmare. Unless?* Echoes of the haunting laughter reverberated in her head, and she desperately hoped it was her imagination gone wild and not one of her fate-dreams.

She rose from bed and opened the shutter, peeking at the few stars paling in the sky. Less than an hour before daybreak, she figured, close enough to dawn for them to get moving. She quickly braided her long red hair and fastened her wrap belt around her tunic. Then her head cocked to a familiar voice resounding from the main room. She hurried out the door and her eyes lit on her cousin. "Wynn."

"Hello, Lee." A mix of road dust and worry lined Wynn's face.

"We've just arrived, rode off as soon as Bran came with word about Uncle Dylan."

Lia raised her brow at Granda and he explained, "I sent Bran straight away to Kilnsgate. Your Aunt Brina and Uncle Finn needed to know, and I thought it best to have a couple more sets o'hands on the journey."

"A couple more sets? Who else?"

Wynn eyed Lia under a tuft of yellow hair. "Kelven's outside tending to the horses."

Wynn's brotherly friend had been away to the southland markets the last visit Lia and Ma made to Kilnsgate, but the visit before that she'd watched in awe as he helped Aunt Brina's mare while she was foaling. He saved the sick horse and her baby when everyone else had lost hope.

"All four of us then?" She was unsure whether to feel relieved or worried about Granda's call for extra hands.

Granda nodded, his face like worn leather set with two sapphires. "And we'll have a bit of an audience. Everyone's a'chatter about Brume and the strange attacks, and with news o'your da, all eyes are watching us."

Lia ground her teeth, already hearing the villagers bellow at the sight of her. A fifteen-year-old girl should be planning for her wedding, not traipsing off into dangerous and forbidden lands.

Well, this girl has more important tasks than sitting on her rump, embroidering a marriage kerchief.

"Still a bit dark, so have some chicory," Granda Luis said. "When you're finished, go and fetch those blends for your da."

Granda limped out of the cottage and Lia poured a mug of the bitter brew. She pushed a platter of rolls toward Wynn, and he helped himself to a couple.

"Your villagers can't be worse than my ma," Wynn said. "She was like some madwoman, packing anything she could grab, hugging me, and swearing all at the same time. And with Da down in Shoneyville selling the harvest, he'll not get word about Uncle Dylan or our trek into Brume for days."

"It's not that simple with the people here, Wynn." Lia's jaw set hard. "You don't know what it's like to be . . . different, and on top of that a girl, just some weakling lass who should know her place, even if her own da suffers in his bed."

"What's wrong with being different?" Wynn said with raised brow. "Talented's more like it, and anyone saying otherwise is too ignorant to care about. Anyway, nobody could think of you as weak; I've seen you with that crossbow. With your marked skill, only thing I'll be using my blade for is to help you harvest herbs."

Kind words, but he'd never understand the frustration of being shunned for dressing like a boy, casting arrows instead of yarn, and cooking up remedies banned by royal law. A young man with a strong farmer's back and enough charm to melt iron, Wynn drew admiration like flowers did bees.

Lia downed her tea and threw on her cloak. "Time to get going."

Outside, she spotted Kelven speaking to Granda. The twig of a boy had grown since she last saw him in the spring. He stood nearly as tall as Wynn and his snug jerkin revealed a broad chest and thick arms. His parents had died a few years before, and though he worked at his uncle's stables training horses, home was with Wynn's family. Aunt Brina doted on him like one of her own, and he repaid his adopted family with undying loyalty. It carried now in his stance, strong and unwavering, as he made ready for Brume.

Kelven glanced at her, catching her stare, and heat rushed to her face. She lowered her head and sped toward Granda's store. Shaking off her momentary distraction, she bounded into the room and to the bag bulging with tea blends and heavy with the jarred salve for Da. She scooped it up with both hands and paused, wondering.

She set the bag back down and touched the pouch hanging against her chest. Her fingers traced the faceted walls of the quartz nestled within, the same glassy stone she'd dropped in Da's salve the night before. The stone warmed to her touch and she sucked in a breath. Last night, her tired mind had denied the truth of its heat, but now her thoughts spun in revelation, and she darted to Grandma's *Grimoire*.

The leather bound book displayed a golden tree on its cover, along with the outlined figures of a girl, a woman, and an elder. Lia opened it and leafed through the pages, barely paying mind to the lavishly sketched trees flipping by.

I know it's in the section covering elemental powers.

She found what she searched for below a drawing of an oak tree, and read the verse:

> *There is an art to the gathering of stones,*
> *A respect and care in retrieving earth's bones;*
> *For within them is stored the marrow of might,*
> *Ignited by a holder who can wield its light.*

"Need any help?" Wynn said as he poked his head in the doorway.

"Uh, no. Be right out." Lia lifted the heavy *Grimoire* and placed it in a cupboard, sliding the beloved book far back on a shelf. *No need to invite prying eyes*, she figured. Then she gathered the bag of concoctions and scrambled from the store.

Her breath caught at the sight of Ma standing next to Merrie, Da's trusty mare. Koun wagged his whole body as Lia approached, his muzzle soaked with milk.

"Your da insisted." Ma's voice held steady, though her chin trembled. "All night he kept whispering 'Lia take Merrie' over and over. I'm sure he figures she was brave for him, she'll be the same for you."

Merrie shook her tawny mane and settled liquid brown eyes on Lia. Lia blinked back the tears threatening to fall. She loved her frisky horse, Shae, but Merrie was much more seasoned and it would be like having a piece of Da with her.

Ma smoothed her hands over her apron. "I packed a good supply of cheese, dried fruit, and salt pork. There's also a skin of Da's mead, if you should need it."

"We'll be back before you know it, Aunt Carin," Wynn said.

Ma nodded and squeezed her nephew's hand. Then she turned to Lia and crossed both hands over her heart. Lia quickly did the same, their special family gesture speaking louder than words.

Ma mounted Shae and called for Koun to follow. The hound barked, the howlish sound strange and haunting, and he peered at Lia with eyes of pure violet.

"Go with Ma, Koun," Lia said, and her heart tugged for him, "Go home."

She'd expected to take Koun on their journey, her loyal companion never far since the day she found him snuggled in a hollowed yew tree in the Bryns. But Granda thought it best he stay behind. Knowing he'd be there for Ma helped ease Lia's disappointment.

The first arrows of dawn promised a clear autumn day, and the small band set off along the main road leaving Rockberg. Just as Lia had dreaded, numerous people gathered close, gawking. Wynn and Kelven drew stares, the sixteen-year-old boys' presence adding fuel to the chatter. The horses slowed through the growing throng, as if walking through the mire. Lia swallowed hard, her every nerve pulled taut as a bowstring.

Among the startled cries and hushed voices came, "'Tis true, they're going in, even the girl." And, "Nothing but a fool's errand. Brume'll swallow them whole, and the Bryn's will still harbor this plague. I say we burn the Bryn groves all the way to the eastern border!" Shouts of agreement resounded.

Lia wanted to yell back, to remind them it wasn't some plague ravaging their people, and burning the groves would do nothing to a root-creature who crept underground. She wanted to shout how Granda knew Brume's mysteries better than anyone alive did. They should trust his wisdom, and know that he'd never lead his kin to their deaths.

She flinched at the shriek of an old woman, "Shame upon the lot of you! 'Tis one thing dabbling in the crafts, 'tis quite another venturing to the cliffs of Brume. You, young lady, have truly gone astray."

Lia held her head up high and her lips pressed in silence, though her insides churned. Why didn't anyone realize it was precisely this "dabbling in the crafts" and "venturing to Brume" that could save them? Had the ignorance of royal rule completely shaded their minds, even while their own people suffered from such blatant attacks?

Granda tilted his snowy head toward the woman. "We'll return before you can wag that finger twice."

The crone's face squinted in reproach, and she stomped away. It was easier for Granda Luis to handle being viewed as an oddity. He was a man, he was an elder, and he was tough as hurr burr root.

Lia ventured a glance to the edges of the crowd and her heart skipped. Some of the villagers raised their hands in farewell. A few had tears shining in their eyes. A handful of wives missing husbands at their side smiled at Lia. One mouthed the words, "Thank you."

Another blew her a kiss. A lump grew in Lia's throat, as she dared to hope for her people's support. She raised her hand and smiled back at them. *They uphold us*, she thought, her tension easing. *They have faith in our quest.*

Then her eyes fell to a group of girls her same age, scowling at her. Lia's insides tightened once more. The girls knotted together, chattering like hens. Lia turned her head from their scorn and swallowed down the retort growing bitter on her tongue.

She cast a glance toward Wynn and Kelven, certain the girls had caught their attention. She wasn't surprised to see Wynn puffed up like a rooster. The girls ogled her cousin while he flipped blond locks from his face. Kelven, on the other hand, aimed his eyes straight ahead. Perhaps lace and gowns did not appeal to him. Perhaps he preferred her pale green tunic and long red braids.

Perhaps, Lia chided herself, *he is focusing on their journey ahead.*

The horses paused in their steps as a few people crowded in front of them. Lia's ears pricked at the grumbling of an elder blacksmith. "Word'll be traveling south about this sickness, bringing the royals up here with their useless rules and cures. The king's high sages got their heads in a bog denying the likes of magic."

Lia stifled a smile at his words.

They made it through town to the open road, leaving the voices of the villagers to fade behind them. The quiet of the town outskirts breathed relief on Lia's nerves. She decided most of her people were as ignorant as grub worms, but she couldn't help hoping they remained safe from further attacks, and that everyone who suffered from the poison held strong until Granda found the cure.

They progressed northwest through the quartz-dotted hills. The glassy towers shone like chiseled ice against the sun's kiss. Lia loved the ancient stones of Rockberg, no matter how much the villagers thought them worthless. She had purposely encircled one of the quartz towers with her garden, confident the plants would enjoy the crystal's reflective light.

She grasped the leather pouch dangling against her chest. Her piece of home, the miniature quartz within gave her comfort, and its strange heat gave her a newfound mystery to ponder.

The day neared its zenith when the hills finally gave way to a vast sweep of grassland. The horses loped onto the plains, running for close to an hour before the band halted at a brook. Lia passed out figs and parsley bread. Everyone ate in silence, as if talking might add too much more to think about.

They rode a few more hours before Dunley Meadow sprawled out in front of them, a blanket of golden stalks bending to the whispering breeze. Lia traversed the edge of the valley every spring with Da, helping him deliver his handcrafted furniture to the seafaring village of Willowbrook. Though the meadow bloomed brighter that time of year, autumn's rich hues shone just as beautifully.

A mountain grew in Lia's throat. Now, instead of crossing the meadow alongside Da, she was crossing it to find a way to save him.

25

"We'll get across the meadowland, then set up camp for the night," Granda Luis called out.

Before long, the northern horizon turned gray and the ghastly wall of fog surrounding Brume grew tall before them. The chilling fog drew gasps of awe, but soon a grim calm took hold, and the small clan plowed quietly along for the rest of the day.

Dusk approached, and Lia glimpsed a shuffle in the tall stalks. A pair of brown-tipped ears jutted into view. She halted Merrie and slid to the ground.

She grabbed her crossbow, held her foot on the stirrup, and pulled the sinewy string back into the catch. With a keen hand and careful aim, she loaded the bolt and hit the trigger. The short arrow found the rabbit within seconds.

She trotted off to claim her prize, casting a quick glance toward Kelven. His brows were raised and his lips slightly parted, and Lia beamed with a marksman's pride.

They set up camp in a small clearing and struck a fire. The ill-fated rabbit met with the spit, and after devouring the savory meat, Lia allowed some of the knots in her stomach to unravel. She unplaited her hair and brushed it until it shone like the flames of their fire.

Kelven sat across from her whittling a piece of wood. He carved with precision, his hands rubbing the wood smooth after each stroke, while the firelight danced little shadows across him. She caught him glancing up at her more than once, his dark hair partially hiding his eyes, and she remembered the first time they'd met when he told her his favorite color was red.

Everything he did, from commanding his horse to the soft tone of his voice to the way he wielded his knife revealed a calm assuredness Lia admired. It was this, she realized, more than his pleasing face and strong arms, which caused the warmth flooding her insides.

He must have several girls back in Kilnsgate pining for him. Or maybe there's already that special one waiting for his return.

"Lee," Wynn said, snapping his fingers in front of her stare.

"I, I was just trying to see what kind of wood he was using." A rush of heat filled her cheeks. Kelven started to speak, but Lia jumped up and scurried from the fire. Her cousin snorted as she dashed into the sea of grasses.

What in blazing stars has gotten into me? She reminded herself of one of those insufferable ninnies back home.

She laid out her bedroll away from the campfire, away from everything but the meadow and the great wall of fog looming ahead. Her embarrassment vanished under the weight of Brume's ominous border. It was both inviting and overwhelming. The more she stared at it, the more it seemed to draw her in, like a rope tugging at her core. Her mother's warning echoed in her head, and a buzz of fear hummed within her.

Had Grandma Myrna felt this same pull before she first entered? Had she longed to discover its mysteries, even while fearing it might swallow her up for good?

Lia tucked lower into the grasses moving serenely in the evening breeze, unlike her insides. She reached into one of her pouches and drew out a tiny root, slipping it into her mouth. The sweet licorice root helped allay her nervous stomach, and she chewed it with vigor.

All her life Brume's mysteries intrigued her, like a distant kinsman bonded by blood, but a stranger in every other way. Now, its misty gates pressed hard upon her eyes, cold and unyielding as it called out to her soul.

The changing of the seasons blew crisp across the meadow and Lia awoke shivering under Ma's woolen cloak. *Not my smartest move to sleep away from the fire.* She'd be sure to add heavier coverings from now on.

Their morning fare consisted of brown rolls and apples, consumed quickly before the small band headed off. They progressed in silence toward the massive wall of fog, its wispy arms reaching out to greet them. With every step closer, the mists devoured more of the meadow and sky, and Lia's nerves dangled on tenterhooks.

Granda Luis halted and turned Dobbin to face his troop. The chilled air tugged at his cloak and swept through his winter white hair. His eyes shone from his face and the young trio drew their horses back a few steps.

"We've a straight and narrow trail ahead. We'll go in single file—"

"A narrow trail?" Lia cut in. "But, I thought it'd be some kind of, well, secret passage or something. How is it that only you and Grandma made it through the fog safely? Why didn't others just follow behind, track your steps?"

"There were many who tried." His voice turned morose. "Even after all m'warnings. Men hovering in the wooded outskirts, creeping in the grasses, waiting till I was snug enough within the fog before charging in behind me, their lives over before I could utter a word. Because you see, as with most gates, there are guards."

Lia's eyes widened. She cast a glance at Wynn, whose jaw hung, and at Kelven whose face was like stone.

Granda Luis added, "But not to worry, our passage was assured long ago."

Lia opened her mouth, but held her tongue as Granda turned Dobbin around and headed him toward the perilous boundary. *Guards? How is that possible?* The notion of it chilled her like an icy deluge. Then the words from the *Grimoire* echoed inside her head:

> *Fogged, bogged gates of Brume, barrier to my home;*
> *Timeless, faceless watchers loom, but I am allowed to roam.*

"Come on, Dobbin. 'Tis all right, boy, steady now," Granda Luis cajoled. Dobbin snorted and flipped his head up and down. "I was afraid o'this. He's strong as a bull, but nervous as a cat, nothing like his fearless sire who'd brazen out the fog without a wink. Come on, boy, walk!" He struggled to move Dobbin forward, but the animal reared and the other horses backed away.

Kelven rode up and neared the anxious horse. "Luis, sir, I think I can help." He dismounted Koby and commanded him with a mere nod, and his mount stood stock-still.

Kelven approached Dobbin and whispered words that Lia couldn't make out. He placed one hand on Dobbin's muzzle and used his other to caress the sorrel-colored mane. Dobbin settled, finally stilled, and whinnied softly. Lia reveled in Kelven's poise, her fears ebbing like a receding tide.

Kelven reached into his leather jerkin and brought out a carrot, feeding it to the calmed animal while he stroked his coat. "If you'll allow me to lead as we go through this fog, we could pull him through to the other side. He'd feel better, I think, following another horse in."

With his brow knitted, Granda Luis replied, "All right, but listen to me carefully; you must stay to the trail, keep your eyes to it at all times, as that's the only way to ensure we don't get lost in the mists. I'll be stopping us mid-way to leave a few offerings."

Well, that might explain the separate pack of ale and bread, Lia surmised. Then she shuddered to think about what sort of creature could subsist in the fog.

Ropes connected the small band, led by Kelven astride his horse Koby, with Wynn and his dapple-gray Nolan bringing up the rear. The procession eased into the mists, and the air turned frigid, like the breath of a cave.

CHRISTINA MERCER

Merrie's ears twitched and she snorted. Light dimmed to mere shadows and Lia barely made out Dobbin's tail swishing in front of her. She pulled her cloak tighter, leaving only her face exposed to the chill. The wall of fog enveloped them, with only the horse's rhythmic hoof beats to break its eerie silence.

No turning back now, Lia thought.

A small golden light shone through the fog and Lia's heart skipped. *Granda's walking staff!* The amber stone that topped it glowed like a sunny orb against the cold gray. *He's done it, he's wielded magic.* It was just like in the verse:

> For within them is stored the marrow of might,
> Ignited by a holder that can wield its light.

Lia placed her palm over her pouched crystal. It warmed against her touch, undeniable this time, another stone treasure waiting to be unlocked.

Before now, Granda had never revealed his use of magic. "Power's in the plants," he'd say with a playful wink, whenever she caught him mumbling over his blends. Then he usually followed it with, "Just gotta know how to ask for it."

Even after all her years of being his trusted helper, Lia still marveled at the way he hovered his hands like loving umbrellas over the herbs, or how he chatted away in the gardens to some invisible audience. She tagged behind him like a puppy, eager to learn, eager to please, prattling away scores of questions. When he stopped and answered her, his words were slow and deliberate, like a steady

32

drizzle of rain seeping deep into the soil.

Lia wondered what other secrets Granda might unveil on this journey. And how many *Grimoire* riddles might finally unravel.

She stared down at the barren strip that made up the trail. Besides the radiant gold shining from Granda's staff, the narrow path was the only thing visible in the gray soup surrounding them. Without Kelven's keen eye to the trail and the ropes connecting them, they'd have no sense of direction. The tangled scrub grass edging the path gave Lia a glimpse of the land hidden beyond. She couldn't imagine much else growing in such gloom.

Their trek drew on, long and dreary, an endless march through the cold murk without incident. The rocking cadence of her horse lulled Lia, and her thoughts began to wander. Certainly, they were getting close to the other side. Perhaps the guards in Brume's fog no longer existed.

She knew Granda hadn't come through in years, and there'd been no word of attempts by others since the soldiers had come to Rockberg. The king's men had lingered long enough to convince most people that Brume was nothing but barren sea cliffs and frozen mountains. Laws forbidding passage had squelched any remaining desire to seek out what might lay in and beyond Brume's fog.

Lia sighed and rubbed her eyes. To stay alert, she sang her favorite tune,

> *Sow, sow, the seeds we sow,*
> *We watch them sprout, we watch them grow;*
> *Hum, hum, the bees do hum,*

For nectar's flow, beneath the sun;
Time—

All at once, the hairs on her neck stood up. The mist's icy fingers turned sharp, grating across her face, and whispers called out to her. A moment later, the air quieted, and she thought her ears must be playing tricks. She continued singing,

—time, it's harvest time,
When the dew has fallen, and the weather is fine—

Her words froze like treacle in her throat as, "Lia . . . Lia . . ." chorused over and over, undeniably real. Fear gripped her gut, her knuckles went white, and her legs turned to water.

A gust of wind whipped past, its force unraveling her hair from the silver bodkin that pinned it. Another gale tore at her face like a razor. Her mind froze in terror. She clawed at her hood, pulling it to block the blasts of air that one after another razed her flesh. It was no use. The treacherous blusters raged against her and the horrid moans became shriller, piercing like knives into her frenzied mind.

She shook her head back and forth, fighting the heavy curtain closing over her thoughts. Merrie snorted and Lia clung to the reins, the leather straps serving as her only anchor. She wondered why her horse wasn't panicking in the storm, and why Kelven hadn't hurried their pace. Perhaps they were all as frozen in fear as she was.

Then, like shreds torn from a midnight sky, ink-black images suddenly swam before her eyes. Their long wispy forms flew like tattered cloth through the roaring winds. *What are they?* They

34

encircled themselves around her in a whirlwind, and Lia's mind grappled to remain lucid.

The whispers grew more urgent, though she could make out none of the words. *Is that laughter in the distance?* She didn't know what was real anymore. A prickling sensation covered her body, as if she'd fallen into a patch of nettles, and the black forms whirled closer around her. *Please, let me be!* Her body fell limp and her mouth tasted like sand, but with a tiny reserve of will, she freed her imprisoned voice. "Nooo!"

A powerful gust slammed against her chest, its force knocking her from Merrie and onto the hard ground. Sparks flashed before her eyes and she struggled to regain her breath.

"In the name o'Myrna, keep to the pact. Take your fare and be off with you." Granda Luis tossed a stuffed pouch into the fog. He dismounted Dobbin and reached his hand down. "Lia, we've got to keep moving."

"I've got her." Wynn jumped to Lia's side, grabbed hold of her, and lifted her back up onto Merrie. Instead of mounting Nolan, he hoisted himself behind his cousin and took Merrie's reins.

Lia shuddered at the maniacal shrieks carried on the dying winds, and "Myrna," the call of Grandma's name, echoed inside her head.

The caravan finally quickened its pace. The world grew quiet and Lia lifted her head. She sucked the air in deeply, calming some of her panic. *They're gone. The black images, the voices, the laughter . . . of what?*

The fog thinned and the sky brightened, and Lia saw past

35

Dobbin's backside to Granda, the amber stone set upon his staff dimmed to a subtle sheen.

"Let's untie here, we've come through," Granda Luis said.

Everyone dismounted the horses. Wynn slid off Merrie first and Lia followed on wobbling legs. She leaned against her mare for support and watched Kelven untie the lead ropes. Dobbin nudged and nickered at his new best friend. A measure of Lia's terror subsided as Kelven stroked the horse's muzzle.

His eyes lifted to her, and he was at her side before her next breath. "Here, let me help."

He drew up the edge of his cloak and dabbed her cheek with it. Lia eyed the bloodstained cloth. She brushed trembling fingers over her flesh and found several raised gashes on her cheekbone. Confusion and fear over what happened in the fog battled with the comfort Kelven gave her.

Granda Luis hobbled over and put a hand on Lia's shoulder. "A bit of holigolde should heal them up without a mark. The Scalach shades are tricksters, fatal sentries to most."

"Shades?" Lia's voice broke from her parched throat. "The guards of Brume are ghosts?"

"Of the darker sort. The Scalach's are ruthless keepers of the gates. They create strange winds, powerful enough to tear a body apart."

Icy fear gripped Lia once more. "Then they were trying to kill me."

"No, m'dear. If that were the case, you'd not be standing here now. You were knocked from Merrie, yes, but I'm guessing they hoped to get your attention." His face softened. "You look an awful lot like her you know, your grandma I mean."

Lia's mind spun in confusion. *Had the shades thought I was Grandma Myrna come back again young?*

"Granda, they knew me, they knew my name."

His brow slammed together. "You heard them speak? They called to you?"

"They screamed at me; I couldn't get them out of my head. Then I saw a bunch of black things, like shreds of cloth."

Shock painted Wynn and Kelven's faces. Lia looked from one to the other. "Nobody else heard them, saw anything?"

Wynn shook his head, but then offered, "I, uh, noticed the winds picking up a bit."

Kelven's eyes softened. "I'm sorry, Lia. I heard nothing until your granda called out for me to halt."

A heavy silence followed. Lia battled with her confusion. The raging winds, the voices, the inky forms, all of it unnoticed by the others. *Why?*

Granda Luis cleared his throat and smiled, though it didn't reach his eyes. "You've given me much to ponder on, child. But for now let us stick to the task at hand and be on our way."

Granda started to turn, but Lia reached out to his walking staff. "Granda, you used magic, made your amber glow like a tiny sun."

"Magic's in the stone, an enchantment set by your grandma. This rare amber was her talisman. She wielded it in the fog to allow passage past the shades. Now, its power imparts the rights of passage to all o'her kith and kin."

"What sort of power would cause them to give way to her, or to us?"

"The offerings o'food and drink are enhanced by the amber. Her stone tenders a kind of enchantment, an illusion that gives the wraiths a momentary pleasure o'tasting the fare as the living can."

Lia wondered at such zealous craving for a moment of pleasure. How bleak the existence of a shade must be. What sort of souls were doomed to such a fate? And why had they focused their attention on her?

Granda Luis changed to a lighter tone. "'Tis a strange place we've entered. You'll find everything you come across more extraordinary than the last. But take heart. You'll be pleased at where we're headed next." He squeezed Lia's shoulder before he limped away, leading them all farther into Brume.

With a queasy stomach and an aching head, Lia ambled on, determined not to let the shades haunt her. They continued on foot with the horses following, Wynn keeping a quiet stride beside her. She fingered the tangles from her hair and decided to let it hang freely down her back.

The air blew mild and clear and the scrubby grassland gave way to woods. Thin, white bark peeled down the trunks of numerous birch trees. Granda Luis stopped at one, placed a flat palm on a smooth section, and after a few moments, began cutting away some of the bark. He did this with several trunks, collecting enough to fill a small pouch.

Lia stopped at several curious blood-red mushrooms growing at the base of one of the trees. Without missing a beat, Granda Luis turned to her. "Fly agarics. They're highly poisonous."

A toad hopped up, swiping an inebriated fly from the top of one of the white-speckled mushrooms. The toad's eyes bulged in delight as it swallowed its drugged prey. Lia wondered how long until the toad fell victim to its meal.

They mounted their horses and continued for another hour to the edge of the birch grove. They came to the crest of a hill where an unexpected sight stretched before them.

"Whoa!" Wynn's surprised voice carried across the great expanse.

Beneath an oddly green sky sprawled a massive meadow, a verdant carpet speckled with colors. The trio gaped in awe while Granda smiled.

"Stay to the path," Granda instructed.

So this was where they'd wildcrafted, Lia mused.

She always marveled at the variety of plant cuttings and rootstocks she knew her grandparents had gathered from Brume. Granda Luis used his skills to transform their gathered treasures into gardens of healing magic that flourished year after year.

They ambled down the pathway and Lia heard giggling. It came from a variety of locations that kept changing. Flashes of light blinked all around, flickering across the vast expanse of the meadowland.

"Does anyone else hear laughter?" she asked.

"Yeah, where's it coming from?" Wynn jerked his head around.

"The laughter comes from those playful lights," Granda Luis said. "Those are the *geancanach*, a breed of tiny fae."

Fae? Lia's heart skipped. "They're faeries!"

ye, faeries, or fae folk as I call them. This is their
meadow; they're protected here, free to care for the
plants. And just look at their garden," Granda Luis
said, sweeping out his hand.

They dismounted their horses, and Lia's eyes roved over the
many blooms. Herbs of every sort, many she'd never seen, spread
before her. A few puffy clouds inched into sight, pink and yellow like
the flowers beneath them.

"The sky . . . it's like a reflection of the meadow itself," Lia said.
She wished Ma could see it. She wished Ma could see all the beauty
that surrounded them. Maybe then she'd understand why Grandma
loved it so much.

"Lovely, isn't it?" Granda said.

Dobbin whinnied and tossed his head as a *geancanach* faery fluttered around his muzzle. They laughed at the befuddled horse and Kelven put a soothing hand on Dobbin's mane. The animal nuzzled his nose against him.

"We'll let the horses graze as they please for a bit. The fae have welcomed them," Granda said.

The animals cropped the lush grass and Kelven planted himself close by them. He tossed aside his cloak and unbuckled his leather jerkin, revealing the creamy undertunic stretched over his chest. Heat ran up Lia's neck and she averted her eyes. Giddiness aside, Kelven's easy manner calmed her. She'd seen him a half a dozen times over the past couple of years, and each visit he impressed her with his horse skills. He broke in stallions, helped the mares foal, and groomed even the plow horses to royal standards. He exuded loyalty and trust, and she imagined he could quiet even the most unruly of people or beasts.

"Hey, whoa, stop that! How'dya get away from these gan-con-ahk, anyway?" Wynn jumped from place to place, fleeing the lights repeatedly bouncing against him. Lia shook her head at her frenzied cousin.

"Follow me, you two," Granda Luis said with a grin. Lia threw off her cloak and followed him.

With the amber-tipped staff catching sunbeams at his side, Granda led them into a glade carpeted with lilac and pink heather. The bell-shaped blossoms that covered the shrubs exuded a sweet aroma and hummed with bees.

"Is it always this warm and the flowers in bloom?" Lia asked, drinking in the paradise with her eyes.

"'Tis a kind o'perpetual spring here, at least in this meadow. As you can see, the fae folk are mighty clever." Granda Luis grimaced as he bent his legs to sit.

The blinking *geancanach* faeries surrounded them and Lia tried to get a closer glimpse of one lighting on the flowers. She stared at a cluster of pink blooms and flinched. What came into view was nothing like the fae of her imaginings. The creature resembled a mantis with bulbous eyes and jagged arms. It wore a cloak of green belted with a blade of grass, and she thought sure it winked at her before it vanished in a flash of light.

Another one landed closer, all hairy legs and fangs, and Lia nearly came out of her boots. The spidery creature wore a cloak of purple, rippling like a flag from its body. "Why are they so dreadful?"

"Train your eye upon them a bit longer," Granda said.

She did what he said, though her insides were coiled like a spring. When another faery landed resembling a toad wearing a blue scarf, she held her gaze on it. Just before it flashed out of view, her eyes captured the truth. The toad changed into a sprite standing a few inches tall with a bronzed face and the same blue scarf wrapped around him. The tops of his pointed ears poked through black hair and his large slanted eyes gleamed viridian.

They're shapeshifters! The fae were clever, indeed.

43

Just then, several fae of a prettier sort fluttered toward them. They landed on the flowers like tiny human butterflies, complete with antennae and large multi-colored wings. They shimmered in mantles of yellow and orange, and unlike the shapeshifting *geancanach*, they were true to their form. They didn't blink in and out of sight, but rested with ease on the blossoms.

Excitement filled Lia as she remembered another verse from Grandma's *Grimoire*:

> *When the flowers do bloom, shiny and bright,*
> *With the colorful tidings of spring,*
> *Here they will come, in a buzz of flight,*
> *Magical pillywiggins.*

"These are pillywiggins," she said, prompting a raised brow from Granda.

Several of the diminutive faeries covered their mouths, muffling high-pitched giggles while they flew alongside the honeybees gathering nectar from the blossoms. A few vexed Wynn by ruffling his hair, pulling his tunic, and fluttering against his face.

"Pilly . . . *what?*" Wynn tried to cover his nose from the enamored creatures.

An unusually large bumblebee with a rider astride it came into view and landed in front of Granda. Everyone took pause as a regal pillywiggin floated off her buzzing mount. Her translucent wings flickered and antennae poked through waves of sable-colored hair. Her skin shone like honey and she wore silk that glimmered like stardust.

"Greetings, Luis. Has it been so long?" The faery's voice came surprisingly loud.

Granda Luis bowed his head in reverence. "Aye, Lady Ebrill, time moves quickly for humankind. You've not changed a bit, as vibrant as ever."

"And these are your kin," she said, her violet eyes shifting to Lia.

Lia drew back. *Those eyes*, she thought, *where have I seen those eyes?*

"Aye, Wynn and Lia are my grandchildren. We've come seeking your help."

"Go on." Her vivid gaze fixed on Lia, as if the faery could reach out and brush the edges of Lia's mind. Lia didn't look away, though her heart thudded.

"My son-in-law and several other villagers have been attacked near Brume's eastern border. A kind o'wild plant bound and poisoned them. They're suffering horribly, our remedies barely helping."

Sadness washed over Ebrill's face and her wings lowered. "The dark power grows stronger as the enchantment weakens; this power is a plague upon your world and ours."

Tears welled up in the faery's eyes. Lia wanted to say something, reach out to her, but Ebrill turned away and fluttered back up to the fuzzy thorax of the bumblebee. "Vile bane, this poison is dark, requiring magic beyond our garden cures. We fae must keep to the protection of our meadow while we still can, but there are those beyond here that may assist you."

"Where?" Granda Luis persisted.

"Start with the tree of your name, good man, the *Luis* tree at the eastern edge of our meadow." Ebrill bowed her head before the bee buzzed her away, followed by a train of colorful attendants.

The *Luis* trees were Granda's namesake, Lia recalled. His birth name was Rowand, taken from the common name of the rowan tree, but his bride preferred the ancient tree names, and he'd gone by Luis ever since.

Lia nibbled on her bottom lip and looked off to the distance, a slow and methodical scan of the wooded horizon. Streaks of gray bled into the fae's green sky where the meadow met with the trees. Her search moved east to a blaze of orange-red, and she knew she'd spotted their destination. Granda Luis stood nearby, his somber face also aimed at the rich fruits of the *Luis* trees.

Their horses munched on the array of plants and even Dobbin seemed to have relaxed, grazing amid the flashes of light. At Kelven's command, all four horses came to attention. The small band mounted them and moved along the trail again.

They crossed a small brook that fed into the meadow, bubbling and foaming over moss-covered rocks. The horses stopped to drink and something shimmery swam beneath the water. It moved like a fish, but it had appendages. Lia peered into the stream and noticed a creature resembling a small woman with green hair and silvery skin that glistened when she moved.

With a splash, Wynn fell from his horse, landing flat on his back in the shallow brook. "Spades! What is it about this place? I feel like a clumsy fool."

Wynn fumbled in the water and the creature swam like a ribbon of silk around him. He struggled to stand up, and she reached out and wrapped her arms about his legs, nearly tumbling him over again.

"Undines, charming water fae." Granda chuckled. "Aye, Wynn, the fae folk do seem to like you. This one appears quite smitten."

Kelven laughed at his befuddled friend, his eyes dancing with amusement. Lia was giggling so hard that when Kelven turned his gaze onto her, a gasp slipped through her lips. But she didn't look away. Their eyes locked and her stomach fluttered like a thousand bees.

"We'll enter the woods on foot," Granda said, snapping them back to attention. "The horses can roam in that patch of clover ahead. Let's just hope we receive the same hospitality in the grove as we have here in the meadowland."

"What do you mean; what's in the grove?" Lia veered Merrie closer to Granda.

Granda Luis looked straight at her and paused, a technique he had often used to claim her full attention, and then he replied, "Trees."

Taken by his solitary word, Lia looked upon the flourish of *Luis* trees. Feathery green leaves and clusters of ripe berries covered their upward-reaching branches. Twitters, twills, and a variety of other birdsong resounded from the woodland, and another memorized verse from Grandma's book sang inside her head:

I know that when I'm under
Your crown of sunny wonder,
Sacred Luis, *luster of my eye,*
I'll find sleeping green serpents
Dreaming of starry fortunes,
And giving courage to those who try.

Lia slipped off Merrie while she reflected deeper on the *Grimoire's* written wisdom. The book abounded with tree lore, entwined within its riddles, recipes, and tales. The leather cover was embellished with one, its crown and roots an image of golden majesty, and drawings of all sorts of trees covered the pages within the book. Of course, trees. So what answers could they find from these autumn-bright *Luis* trees?

It took Wynn's grumbling to break into Lia's thoughts. She smirked in amusement as he secured his sword to sodden breeches. Though he looked a mess, his blade was encased in the most beautifully engraved scabbard—a creation of Kelven's.

It was pointless to tote her crossbow into such a dense thicket, so she decided to leave it behind. She wove her hair into two long braids to keep it from snagging in the branches. Her knapsack remained flung over her back, numerous pouches hung from her wrap belt, and she kept her seax—her working knife—at her side.

Kelven released a dirk from another glorious scabbard. Lia's eyes flickered from his blade up to his chiseled face. "Where'd you get such a beautiful blade?"

He grinned at her. "I, uh, traded for it." He held back a few

48

branches for Lia to go ahead of him. She smiled and brushed by him ever so softly. He sucked in his breath and then cleared his throat, and Lia's smile broadened.

"The village swordsmith's a good friend. He liked my saddlebags and I liked his knife, though I think I came out ahead on the bargain."

"Oh, I don't know about that." She ducked beneath the tangled trees. "The saddlebags you've brought with you are the finest I've seen, and so are the scabbards. Have you always been so crafty with leather?"

They followed her limping granda slowly through the grove, and though Lia listened for Kelven's reply, her eyes stayed keen on the trees. The air grew cool, as if spring had turned its back, and she knew with growing wariness that they'd left the warm cradle of the fae.

"Well, my uncle taught me some basics when I was young and I just kept going from there. I like working the material; it relaxes me, almost as much as training horses."

They maneuvered through the copse of entwined trees and Lia was sure everything dimmed in color. She shivered and regretted not bringing her cloak.

"I know what you mean. It's like working with the herbs for me." She hunkered through the dense foliage. The woods took on a musky scent, like fresh-turned soil, though the leaves and undergrowth blanketing the ground appeared dry and untouched. "I love working with the plants, love making up tea blends and oils."

Kelven's footsteps crunched close behind her. "Yours is a rare craft these days, thanks to our blundering rulers, and one that should always be kept alive."

Lia warmed at his words. "Guess it helps being so far north, keeps the king's men from nosing around too much."

She followed the rough trail Granda and Wynn had blazed. A strange sensation pricked at her senses, and she paused in her steps.

"What is it?" Kelven whispered behind her.

Lia eyed the surrounding woods for movement or sound, but found only the chilled breeze and birds flitting about. "I, uh, guess it's nothing."

Her mood turned edgy and she hurried her steps through the tangled grove. Kelven kept with her pace and quiet concentration. She shivered, more than eager for their trek through the woods to end. Then she stopped short when she plunged into a clearing.

Lia's eyes widened on the unusually large *Luis* tree growing alone in the middle of the open area. A resonant caw called from one of the branches. The black bird took flight, swooping low before it shot into the gray sky.

At Granda's prompting, they drew closer to the tree. Granda Luis placed his hand on the smooth, silvery bark. Lia's insides buzzed with wonder. After a few moments of silence, there came a rustling among the dried leaves at the base of the tree. Lia's breath caught as a yellow-green creature with the body of a snake and the head of a dragon emerged from the leaves and slithered up the trunk.

Wynn and Kelven both jumped forward with brandished blades.

"Stand back," Granda Luis called out. "The tree wyrm is here to help us."

Tree wyrm? Lia planted her eyes on the mysterious creature. Wynn and Kelven reluctantly lowered their weapons and took a few steps back.

The creature moved easily, and its luminous scales glistened as it wrapped around the trunk of the tree. Several teeth poked out from its long snout and a row of spines ran down its forehead between sparkling green eyes. Ear frills fanned out like veined leaves on each side, and above them, a pair of horns branched back from his brow. Granda Luis leaned against his staff as the creature raised his head.

"Friend to the fae," a voice uttered.

It speaks! Lia's heart raced. *But wait, its mouth didn't open. How . . . ?*

Granda Luis replied, "Greetings. Lady Ebrill sent us to seek your wisdom about a creature breaking through the eastern border. Barbed roots are attacking and poisoning our people."

"Ah, yes, the *Straif.* She creeps underground, finds her way through," the smooth voice carried through Lia's mind.

Ohhh, it's using mindspeak!

She turned wide eyes on Granda and he gave her a glance and quick nod of confirmation. Then she jerked her head around to Wynn and Kelven. Their hands remained on the hilts of their blades and confusion lined their brows. Neither were apparently privy to the creature's silken replies.

"What must be done? How do we find a cure for her poison?" Granda Luis continued.

The creature paused and turned its iridescent eyes to Lia. She stumbled back and nearly lost her footing, but remained focused on the tree wyrm. Its huge mouth remained clamped shut, only the heat from its nostrils pouring forth, as its voice crooned on, "The guardians are losing power. Darkness devours the veil. The *Great Nion* is where you must go."

Granda Luis stood quiet, as if waiting for more, but the creature remained silent. Finally, Granda let out a sigh and replied, "Many thanks, Wise One. Lia girl, fetch some dragonwort for our friend."

"Uh, yes." She swung around her pack and reached into it. After some searching, she brought out a black, knobby, S-shaped root. Carefully, she held it out to the tree wyrm who took it into its mouth.

"The fruits are yours," the tree wyrm imparted, before slithering down the tree and out of sight.

"Wynn, cut some of those berry clusters down," Granda Luis said before he limped back toward the thicket. Kelven gave Lia a nod and jogged to her granda's side, helping to move branches out of the elder's path.

Wynn hacked down several clusters of *Luis* berries, handing them to Lia. She packed them up and hurried after Granda and Kelven.

"What in ruddy spades was that all about?" Wynn said, following her.

"You didn't hear it, did you? That tree wyrm spoke in our heads."

"Wait, that snake-creature used mindspeak?" Wynn plowed through the undergrowth to walk beside her.

"Yes, and to think those *wise royal sages* sitting fat in the palace say it can't be done. 'Delusions of the crazed'," she mocked. "What blatherskites."

"What did it say?" He pushed aside the twisted branches.

"The roots attacking are from a *Straif*, and we have to seek out the *Great Nion* for the cure," she answered.

"Strah-f? Nee-uhn? And you understand all this?"

"They're trees. *Nion* is an ash and *Straif* is the ancient name for the blackthorn."

"So, a tree attacked your da?"

"Not just any tree, Wynn. The thorny blackthorn is tricky enough without magic. I can't imagine what an enchanted one could do." She paused and then recited a passage from the *Grimoire*,

> *Baneful* Straif, *tree of strife;*
> *Wicked thorns cut like a knife.*
> *Beware its roots in their menacing twist;*
> *Beware jagged pricks from this arrow of the mist.*

Wynn shook his head as if he'd missed the point.

Lia added, "All trees carry some sort of lore, ancient legends passed down. The *Straif's* are mostly about pain and war. The old tribes used its tough wood to craft cudgels—special fighting clubs—

and its thorns to make deadly spear points."

Her words stopped as they neared Granda Luis and she caught the change in his gait. *His knees must be flaring up*, she thought, and knew the stubborn man would keep stumbling through the woods with no reprieve. She'd have to feign an excuse to stop him.

But before she could utter a word, he collapsed to the ground.

Deadwood

"G randa!" Lia tore through the grove to his crumpled body. "I've got him." Kelven lifted him up.

Granda Luis sputtered, "Wretched . . . bramble," and then passed out.

Kelven held him tight and glanced at Wynn. "Let's each take a side, might be gentler on him that way." Wynn positioned himself on one side and they carried Granda ahead.

Lia remained frozen to her spot. *Wretched bramble?* She bent down to retrieve Granda's walking staff, peering at the ground, unable to shake the dread washing through her. She studied the thick carpet, finding only decomposing tree fall and patches of moss.

The amber orb suddenly grew bright, a golden aura emanating outward for a moment. Lia carefully lifted the staff from the leaves.

The honeyed stone was knocked askew. She placed her hand on it, and her eye caught something through the glassy resin. With a deft finger, she probed under the stone into the hollow of the staff and pulled out a scroll.

"Lee," Wynn called back.

"I'm coming." Lia stuffed the rolled parchment within the folds of her tunic, set the amber in place, and hurried ahead.

They made it out of the coppice and found a spot between the stream and clover patch to settle. The day had waned into twilight, though the fae meadow continued to glow with its flashing lights.

"I'll get a fire going," Kelven said, and he scrambled away to collect wood.

Lia laid out a bedroll and Wynn settled Granda down onto it. With a long exhale, Wynn turned stormy eyes on Lia. "Have his legs ever given out like that before?"

"He has flareups all the time, swelling and pain, but I've never seen him collapse. Maybe he's overdone himself. I'm sure he's exhausted." She refused to panic. "The usual remedies, some food when he wakes, a good night's sleep, should do the trick."

Her cousin's grim look improved. "All right then, I'll be back," he said, and left her to tend to Granda.

Lia was soon pinching several herbs into the kettle while Kelven stoked the fire.

"What are you making?" he asked.

She met his eyes. "An infusion of Granda's favorite. Bridewort helps the swelling and featherfew eases the pain."

"Huh. And what's in the linen?" Kelven pointed to a pair of bundled cloths.

"The poultices are for his knees. A blend of arnica, knitbone, and holigolde."

He raised his brow. "You've really got the knack."

A smile tugged at Lia's mouth. She was glad she knew the healing crafts, glad she could help Granda. And glad that Kelven upholded such skills.

Wynn rushed up to the fire just then with a spear full of trout and a grin stretched across his face. "That undun, undee, oh spades, that water faery helped me. She corralled them in a cove while I speared away."

Lia shook her head. Sometimes her cousin's charms paid off.

She put the kettle over the flames and prepared the fish, using a salt and oil rub before frying the catch. She kept a keen eye on Granda while they ate, and when he finally stirred, she hurried to his side with a mug of the herbal infusion.

"Ah, girl, you know . . . just what . . . to do." Granda Luis winced as Wynn helped him into a seated position. "Thank you, my boy. Lia, the *Beth* bark, would you fetch it from my pouch?"

Beth was the ancient name for a birch tree, Lia recalled. She jumped to his bidding and returned with the pale bark that he'd gathered that morning, along with the hot poultices. She knelt down and glanced at his walking staff lying at his side. "Granda, back in the grove where you fell, the amber stone shone for a moment."

"That's odd," he muttered, his face drawn and pale. "Never lights up unless the shades are about."

Lia's breath caught in her throat. "Shades?"

"Couldn't be, really," Granda mumbled. "The Scalach's are bound to the fog. Perhaps the amber's grown a bit touchy from its years away from Brume." Granda set his mug of tea down and then carefully dragged up one side of his ragged breeches.

Lia reached out to assist him and her mouth fell at the sight of his swollen knee. Then she spotted the green sores speckled along his calf. "Granda, those wounds . . . they're like Da's."

"The bark, its pulp," Granda Luis wheezed between clenched teeth.

"Uh, of course." Lia willed her hands to stop trembling as she placed the pain-relieving *Beth* pulp around his swollen knee. She placed the hot poultice over the pulp and tied everything together with a strip of nettle cloth. She salved the tiny pustules in his calf while Granda fortified himself with another gulp of tea. In fearful silence, she moved to his other leg, slathering his knee and the green sores running up his leg with waxy salve.

After she finished, he grumbled softly, "It got me, girl. Somehow that wily *Straif* got me. This meadow, the fae's magic, 'tis holding the worst of the poison at bay. But for how long, I can't tell."

His chilling words seeped like snowmelt inside Lia's mind and she gulped down a surge of dread. She wanted to deny it, but knew he spoke true. She had felt something horrid lurking back in those woods, and the amber's magic had confirmed it.

"Cunning blackthorn, wretched tree," Lia cried. She shot looks at Wynn and Kelven, their faces both tight with worry, and then she blurted, "Granda, the only way I see it now is we split up, two of us go on to the *Nion* tree to find the cure—"

"No!" he roared before a fit of coughs racked his body.

Lia patted his back and Kelven lifted a water skin to his lips. Granda Luis calmed and then placed his timeworn hands over his eyes. Lia couldn't remember ever seeing Granda weep and the sound of his hushed sobs nearly shook her apart.

"Lia girl, this journey is over, do you hear?" His voice cracked. "Best we can do is gather as many herbs as the fae will allow. I'll not endanger your lives more than I already have. Even if I weren't ailin', we'd not be venturing any farther, especially not to seek out the *Nion*. 'Tis a wonder your Grandma escaped it."

The young trio froze at his words. Lia's head spun with the notion that the *Nion* was something to fear, a danger Grandma had to escape.

Granda Luis continued in a low, but commanding voice, "She was young then, raised by a couple of old widows tucked deep in the Bronach Mountains bordering Brume's fog." He wiped his muslin sleeve across his face, smudging dust-filled tears across the wrinkled terrain. "I met her while traveling with Lloyd. He was a doctor-in-training and claimed the old widow women, 'mystic hags' he called them, had the most effective treatment for the ague.

"Your grandma captivated me from the moment I saw her hanging herbs to dry, with her hair like fire, and a look in her eyes as if she held a treasure-trove of secrets. 'Twas only after we married, when she brought me to the gates o'mist, that I witnessed her gift. Your grandma could have gone by several names: seer, diviner, spirit mage."

"Spirit mage?" Lia stumbled on her words. "Grandma spoke with the dead?"

Granda Luis looked directly into her wide eyes and smiled. "Aye, and so can you, my girl. 'Twas you the shades spoke to."

Lia shivered in remembrance of the shades. Yes, she'd heard them, heard their awful moans, even saw their black figures, but it hadn't dawned on her it was because she'd inherited some kind of gift.

Lia cast a glance toward Wynn, sitting wide-eyed and silent, and then to Kelven who held his focus on the fire.

"Mindspeak, another gift," Granda continued. "Took years o'practice under the tutelage o'your grandma and the fae before I could hear any thoughts, and even then, 'twas only with the most skilled creature making up for m'slack. Yet, you had no trouble hearing the tree wyrm. And those little prophetic dreams of yours are not what you'd call a common talent."

Lia felt short of breath, but Granda Luis continued on, now with a sense of urgency, rattling off tales until his voice waned thin. The ungilded truth was what she had always wanted, what she'd always pestered him for, but now her head felt like bursting. When Granda finally collapsed into slumber, desperation drove her from the campfire to the embrace of the meadow.

The cooler air helped clear her thoughts and she drew in deep breaths, one after another, each one easing the weight on her mind. In the short hours of twilight, Granda's words shattered all doubt, all uncertainties about Grandma Myrna's magic. And now her own. Grandma's *Grimoire* went from a book of invaluable remedies and wondrous fables to a powerful treasure of truth. A truth Lia struggled to grasp all at once.

Wynn jogged up behind her. "Hey, Lee, you all right?"

She averted her eyes. "I just needed some air."

"You know, you're not alone."

"I know you worry for Granda, too, Wynn."

"No, you don't understand. I mean, you're not alone in inheriting Grandma's gifts. Holly has visions."

Lia's eyes grew wide and she faced him. Wynn's younger sister had, "Visions?"

"They started back in the spring. They were little things she'd know before they happened, when she touched one of us or something we'd held. A couple days before we got word of your da, she handed me my sword and told me I'd be going far away."

Lia's head spun with this added revelation. "She's touch-scrying. There's a few passages in the *Grimoire* about it. The ancient mountain tribes honored their scryers, used them to track people or foretell a warrior's success in battle. Holly's gift is special, yet another strange inheritance."

They both went silent while the fae danced around them like fireflies. Then Lia added, "Hope it's easier for her with visions. Sometimes it's hard to tell with fate-dreams what's real and what's not. Like the dream I had of you a few nights ago."

"Oh?" His brow lifted.

"It was absurd really, a vision of you trekking through a clouded forest, and you had, well, jagged white streaks in your hair. Sounds odd, I know, probably why I didn't give it much thought."

"White streaks, huh? Hope it was only a dream or I'm aging faster than I thought." Wynn gave her a strained grin. "Anyway, I guess I realize now what you meant about being *different,* and Holly must feel the same."

Concern etched across Wynn's face and he jabbed his toe into the soil. A sudden pang shot through Lia for Holly. She wondered what other skills her young cousin might harbor. What else did the eleven-year-old girl hold secret, too bewildered or afraid to speak about?

"When all this is over and you get back home," Lia said, "you tell Holly that she is not alone, not ever, and it's high time she come for a stay with me."

Some of the lines on his brow smoothed. He started to turn and then asked, "Do you have any idea what happened to Grandma's parents?"

"No." Lia shook her head. "The only mention of them is a short verse in her book that reads,"

> *Parents gone but never forgot,*
> *For they leave a legacy*
> *Of honeyed drops floating nobly,*
> *Upon a rich velvet sea.*

Wynn shook his head and shrugged, and they made their way back to the fire. Kelven had taken his bed closer to the horses, and Lia wondered what thoughts ran through his mind. She hoped he still looked at her with those soft hazel eyes and tender smile come morning.

Lia settled into her bedding, but struggled to relax under the moon hovering above. She and Holly, the only granddaughters, bore Grandma's mysteries. Their mothers hadn't any gifts, at least none either of them acknowledged. Perhaps the magic skipped a generation. So, what of the only grandson, Wynn? Did the fact that he was a male preclude him, or did he harbor an undiscovered skill?

Lia soaked up the warmth of the flames, wondering why she shivered in the spring-like air. She glanced at Granda's sleeping body and murmured, "Sneaking *Straif*, baneful tree, somehow, someway, your venom will be overcome."

As the chorus of snores sang around her, Lia brought out the creased scroll from within her tunic. *All this time Granda's staff harbored a secret.* She unrolled the vellum and immediately recognized the writing upon it. It was the same script, the same ink, with the

63

parchment jagged along one edge. *Why had he torn it out? Why had he hidden away this page from the* Grimoire?

A twinge of guilt ran within her, but she felt too compelled to stop. The firelight blazed on its surface, and she read the poetic verse:

> *A child of imposing grace will shine for all the land;*
> *From moon to moon she will race, as armies take their stand.*
> *Across the kingdom her foe will chase,*
> *As her soul strives to stay free,*
> *And in the end her freedom resides*
> *Within the great hallowed tree.*

Lia read the riddle once more before she tucked it back within the lining of her tunic. For hours, she lay in silence. She worried for Da and Granda, she struggled to find meaning in the riddle, and she pondered on her newly discovered gifts. Tears of frustration streamed down her cheeks and she hid her face in her ma's cloak, shutting out everything but the warmth and softness of its velvet lining, until sleep finally swept her away.

"Lee, wake up!" Wynn's voice cut through her slumber.

Lia woke muzzy-headed, her eyes squinting in the dawning light.

"It's Granda; he's sweating pretty bad."

She threw off her bedding and leapt up to tend to him. "Quick, Wynn, use my blade to get his breeches loose." She handed him her seax knife and rummaged through her knapsack, tossing herb pouches hither and thither.

Wynn gripped the blade's curved hilt and cut the fabric, careful not to graze Granda's swollen legs. Granda Luis moaned and his arms began to flail.

64

"Hold him still." Lia scooped out a heap of salve and rubbed it over the seeping eruptions. The speckled lesions had mutated into hideous sores, now identical to those found on Da. The fae's protective magic was failing against the poison of the *Straif*.

Lia trembled as she prepared a strong sleeping decoction, comprised mainly of vandal root and hops. It took some time to get the hot liquid down Granda's throat, though his face and mouth were less swollen than Da's had been. Thank the stars for the fae's magic. He dozed off, his breathing ragged, but strong. With Granda settled, Lia grabbed hold of her knapsack and sped off toward the horses.

"Lee, wait up! What . . . where are you going?" Wynn hurried behind her.

"I've got to find something we can use. This meadow's full of plants I've never seen before. There's gotta be something that'll work, something to diminish that awful poison."

"What about that faery Granda spoke to, Ebrill?"

The duo immediately retrieved their horses from the clover patch, Wynn yelling for Kelven to watch over Granda. Kelven's eyes met Lia's, and for a split second, time halted. No more panic, no fear, only the warmth of his eyes.

He rushed toward her and her throat went dry. "We have to speak with the fae," she managed to say. "Granda's worsened."

Kelven nodded and brushed his hand across hers. "I'll go and keep watch over him."

Lia and Wynn were soon amid the bright heather. "*Ura*," Lia mouthed, remembering its ancient name. After reaching the same spot as before, they sat until their legs were sore and the sun crested high above. The *geancanach* lights blinked all around them, but the pillywiggins remained out of sight. Frustration twisted Lia's insides until her stomach was one big knot, and Wynn paced through a layer of soil.

Perhaps their efforts were futile, the fae too busy with their own tasks to bother with them further. Maybe they'd become unwelcomed now that Granda was infected by the *Straif*. Had the fae shunned them? What if they turned against them? Panic started to bubble up Lia's throat. Images of what they might shapeshift into ran through her mind.

Then a plump bumblebee hovered down and Ebrill dismounted on the blooms in front of them. Relief pooled within Lia.

"The *Straif* attacked Granda," she blurted. "Please, there must be something we can gather in the meadow, something as strong as we'd find at the *Nion*."

"Lia," Ebrill boomed in her ever-loud voice. "Listen to me. The poison you fight is dark magic, a magic we fae work day and night to keep from harming our meadow. Our plants provide only a part of the remedy needed. If the tree wyrm pointed you to the *Great Nion*, than that is where you must go."

"But how? Granda said it's too danger—"

"You *must* go on. Remember who you are, child. You have the blood of your grandmother and the heart of her gifts." Ebrill's violet

66

eyes flashed. "Don't you understand? This is the only way to save them. This is the only way to save us all."

Split

L ia brandished her knife. "Follow me," she said to her cousin.

Ebrill had instructed her on a few key plants to slow the poison's effects. Wynn stuck close to Lia's side, packing the cuttings of flowering stems and dirt-crusted roots that she handed him. She buzzed through the meadow, harvesting small portions from each cluster of herbs, careful to ensure little stress to the plants. Along with the herbs, she gathered an ample stock of soup greens.

"That should do it," she said, stifling the fear that stirred within her. "Enough to leave with Granda and Kelven, and a good supply for my pack."

They arrived back at camp in a hushed frenzy, and Lia sorted healing concoctions while Wynn divided food and supplies.

"Are either of you gonna tell me what's going on?" Kelven's

voice was calm, but worry engraved his brow.

"Follow me," Lia whispered. She led both boys a fair distance from the camp, and then turned to Kelven. Heat rose up her neck despite her distress. "We have to split up. Wynn and I are going on to find the *Nion* tree."

"You...you're going on?"

Wynn placed his hand on Kelven's shoulder. "We need you to stay with Granda."

"I, of course, I'll do whatever you need." Kelven's eyes flickered from Wynn to Lia. "Let me go with Lia in your stead."

"No, Kel, I have to go," Wynn said. "I have to follow this through for my kin. See what you can do to get Granda back home. If we're not back by the week's end, you'll need to get word to Kilnsgate, to Ma."

"The amber on Granda's staff and an offering of food should get you through that fog," Lia said, warmed by Kelven's desire to go with her. "Aside from their interest in me, the shades held to the pact. Like Granda said, the amber's enchantment imparts passage to all of her kith and kin."

Lia didn't have to mention how she and Wynn planned to get back. The previous night's revelations had divulged her power to them all. But her newfound gift as a spirit mage terrified her. She held to the notion that Grandma Mryna had found a clever way to deal with the shades. When the time came, Lia would find a way to use her gift with ghost-speak to do the same.

Granda slept soundly while Lia rolled up her bedding. She took heart that at least sleep eased his suffering, and Kelven would be there with the brew she made when he woke. She bent down and kissed his forehead, forcing back tears. Granda had to hold on now, too, while she and Wynn did whatever it took to bring back the cure.

Granda's words from the night before echoed in her mind, "The *Great Nion* grows at the crest of a cliff, overlooking the sea." He went on to describe how Grandma Myrna, as a curious youth, trekked the lower mountains and came on the largest tree she had ever seen. Awed by its sheer size and majestic canopy, she ventured near enough to hear a cacophony of ear-wrenching cackles. The hideous laughter, the sight of a black snake coiled at her feet, and a frightful force wrapping around her mind like a sticky web, prompted her to flee and never return.

While Wynn fetched their horses, Lia finished her preparations and cinched her knapsack shut. She set it on her bedding as Kelven approached. "I emptied my saddlebags for you. You'll have more space and they'll withstand any kind of weather. I strapped a few short spears inside, might come in handy for fishing or as skewers."

Lia lifted her eyes to his. "Thanks, I mean, really, Kelven, thank you for everything. It's been, well, you've been—"

"Just come back in one piece, all right?" Kelven brushed wisps of coppery hair back from her face. His thumb traced the shade-inflicted wounds fading on her cheek, and a ripple of heat ran through her.

"I've never felt . . . I wondered if you—" Lia whispered.

"I feel the same. Have for years, waiting, hoping Wynn's fiery cousin would think of me." Kelven pulled her closer. His hands trembled on the small of her back. Lia wondered if he could hear the thumping of her heart.

He lowered his head and brushed his lips down her cheek, hesitating for a heartbeat. Lia lifted her chin, and Kelven kissed her on the mouth, lingering in a moment of sweetness. Lia had never felt so exhilarated and pained at the same time.

Their embrace ended at the sound of horses approaching. With Kelven's breath warm on her face, Lia turned away. She could only hope they'd reunite soon.

Lia and Wynn sped northwest from camp. It took the remaining hours of daylight to traverse the meadow. To Lia's relief, Wynn said nothing about Kelven and her. Perhaps he hadn't seen their embrace after all. Kelven's kiss still burned on her lips. The thought of him left her giddy, yet comforted. She'd carry him in her memory for as long as it took until they all returned home.

She glanced south to the distant *Beth* grove where they first entered Brume. It had only been yesterday when they arrived and three days since Da's attack. *Thank the stars he's so strong—strong as an oak tree and nothing, not even that* Straif's *venom, will take him without a fight.* She clung to the notion that Ebrill's herbs would ensure that Granda held strong as well.

They edged the dense wood as night approached, and Wynn

turned Nolan around. "No way to get through that forest now. Have to wait till first light."

Lia nodded, peering at the dark thicket. *The fae meadow has certainly walled itself in*, she thought, *and the rest of Brume is a hidden mystery beyond.*

She slid off Merrie and unstrapped her bedding. The horses wandered to a patch of grass and quieted under the evening sky. Lia wished she could rest that easily. Her body refused to unwind and her mind fretted for what lay beyond the meadow.

The gentle rhythm of a nearby stream called to her, offering a reprieve from the wave of fear gripping her insides. She tossed down her bedroll and grabbed her knapsack. "I'll be back," she said.

She jogged to the banks of the stream and knelt down. In one quick motion, she threw off her tunic and trousers, and slipped into the waters. She dunked her head under, holding her breath until her lungs nearly burst. Though it didn't wash away her worries, the water helped ease the pent-up tension in her body.

With a measure of renewed calm, she grabbed her bag and retrieved a bar of soap that Ma had made. Nothing else compared to its froth of bubbles and sumptuous scent. Villagers from all around sought out the soaps, and Da sold crates of them along with his handcrafted furniture whenever he travelled to the markets.

Lia rubbed the foam over her skin and the scent of honey and elf leaf transported her home. She lathered her hair and then dunked back under the water. As she lifted up, she noticed green hair intermingled with her own red locks.

"Oh!" She pulled back at the sight of a water fae washing in the milky bubbles. The otter-sized undine slipped close, preening her tresses. She rubbed and stroked her green hair. Lia grinned. Hair was the one vanity she could relate to; she cared nothing for the pomp of frills or trinkets, but her long coppery hair had always been her glory.

The faery giggled and disappeared into the brook, and Lia dressed and walked back to camp.

"Feeling better?" Wynn asked, divvying some food from their stores.

She nodded and rolled out her bedding, uninterested in the crusty bread and hunk of yellow cheese Wynn set out for her. She pulled her hair up in a twist, pinning it with her bodkin, and adjusted the leather thong hanging around her neck.

"Whuf's fhat?" Wynn asked, spitting breadcrumbs and pointing to her neck.

"Oh, this?" Lia pulled on the thong and brought out the pouch from beneath her tunic. She opened it and dropped the crystal onto her palm, immediately feeling the strange heat it exuded. "It's a piece of quartz from back home."

"Whatdja do, chisel a piece off one of Rockberg's boulders?" Wynn shoved a hunk of cheese into his mouth.

"No, I, hmm, now that you mention it, it does seem odd. Koun brought it to me in my garden, near the quartz tower that sets there." Concern pricked at her. The more she thought about it, the surer she was that none of the crystal towers of Rockberg had ever cast off

73

pieces before. The monoliths had stood unchanged for as long as anyone could remember. The royals had claimed they were a simple fluke of nature, serving no real purpose, and since you couldn't chop them down like a tree, they were best left alone.

"Haven't those stones been there forever?"

"Well," Lia said, shifting her thoughts, "there's a fable that tells of dwarfs inhabiting our land. For centuries, they guarded and cared for the stone towers, but then our people came and pushed their race far into the northern mountains. Almost overnight the wall of fog appeared, closing them away from humankind, inside this land we call Brume."

"Dwarfs? What a load of muck," he said with a yawn. "About as believable as faeries."

Lia shook her head at him and snuggled into her covers, but in her silence, she contemplated his words. She thought of the fabled dwarfs dwelling in the hills of Rockberg, tending to the crystals, including the one in her garden. She gripped her pouch, the miniature quartz inside becoming more precious by the day. Then she closed her eyes and slipped into dreams of icy mountain caverns.

They rose at first light to warm, sweet air wafting across the meadow. Though they set off in a hurry, the near impenetrable forest slowed them. Merrie snorted as her mistress pulled her through the bracken and scrub, and Wynn swore like a fishmonger as he hacked through the dense brush. The long, tedious trek went on for hours, scraping and scratching, whipping at their faces and hands, until Lia's mood turned as raw as her skin.

Then almost at once, the trees and undergrowth thinned and they were able to mount their horses. Lia pulled her cloak tight in the chilled air, the fae boundaries left far behind.

"There's a clearing up ahead. I think we're coming out of the woods." Wynn hurried Nolan's pace. "Whoa! What in spades?"

Lia charged Merrie up behind him, halting her at the edge of the barren landscape that stretched out before them. The sky loomed overhead, a swirl of cold gray to match the desolate ground below. She rubbed at the sudden droplets of rain pelting her face. Merrie flicked her head, snorting in the fusty air.

Lia slid from her horse and grabbed her crossbow. She held her foot in the metal stirrup jutting from the front of the bow, and spanned the string to the catch. "Best to be prepared," she said, remounting Merrie. With the grove behind them, she wanted her weapon readied. Now, she could fit a bolt and shoot it on horseback.

"We need to get across this flat to the mountain range." Wynn waved her to follow as Nolan bolted ahead.

Lia tightened up her cloak and loosened the reins on Merrie, galloping her across the grotty terrain. Lightning flashed across the sky and the plain left no buffer against the winds. She kept her head bent, and she shook with cold under her woolen layers.

"Let's get up that trail, see if we can find cover." Wynn's voice barely carried across the wind. The narrow trail twisted up a steep ridge. A few ledges provided dismal barriers from the storm.

They climbed for hours before finding a deep enough alcove to tuck into for the night. The exhausted pair dismounted their horses, and the animals huddled close to the mountainside.

"We can at least lay out our cloaks to dry. The bedrolls should be all right, thanks to Kelven's saddlebags," Lia said, eager for her warm covering. Her heart tugged at the thought of Kelven. She pulled off her sodden cloak and wrung out the water from her hair.

Wynn retrieved their blankets and the pouch of jerked venison. "Kel treats the leather with this concoction of oils, rubs it down until it's completely waterproof." He wiped his face and shag of yellow hair with his blanket and then laid it across his lap.

He leaned back and gave Lia a sideways glance. "So, you and Kel, huh? Saw that heart he made you."

Lia's stomach flipped and she bit her lip. "What heart?"

"Etched on the saddlebag, underneath the flap."

Lia got up and stepped over to Merrie. She lifted the front flap of the closest bag and her breath caught. A heart containing the letter 'L' embellished the soft leather. She sat back down and grabbed the bag of jerky, tore off a large piece, and handed it to Wynn. "Eat your supper," she clipped, and he grinned like a fox.

She smiled inwardly and covered up with her blanket, wishing for a steaming mug of her evening brew—maythens and melissa blended with a hint of catmint. At least she was drying off, and the deer jerky filled her mouth with salty satisfaction.

"Thankfully, the *Nion* tree is on the first leg of these mountains.

If we don't get pummeled again tomorrow by the storm, we should make it to the crest by nightfall," Wynn said. "Just hope the sea cliffs aren't much farther west from there."

"Hm-hmm." Lia leaned her back against the wall of stone and tried to relax.

After hours of pelting rain and howling winds, the world finally went quiet. The peace lasted until dawn when Lia opened her eyes to a monster.

Lumber

The rock giant peered down at Lia from black pits that rested above a bulbous nose and cave-like mouth. Rough and craggy, he towered over their shelter with the height of five men. The creature's flesh seemed to crumble when he moved, pebbles and dust tumbling from his pores. In one massive fist, Wynn's sword resembled a dagger, and in his other hung two sets of horse leads.

"Grmf Ezak Grk!" His voice grated against Lia's ears, and her mind scrambled in fear.

The rock giant pointed a finger and motioned for her to move. She shook in horror, carefully rose, and stepped out of the crevice. Wynn stood near with his hands bound in what appeared to be vines.

"Frmp Ompa Slrk!" The giant waved his hand, gesturing for Lia and Wynn to walk ahead of him. He yanked on the horse leads and

Merrie neighed loudly, the mare flipping her head up and down while Nolan bucked and snorted. None of their protesting did any good. They either followed in obedience or found themselves dragged up the mountain.

Surprisingly, Lia's hands remained unbound, though the small freedom made escape no less impossible. The narrow path closed her in, a tight leash held Merrie, and even if she could get to her crossbow hanging from the saddle, her sharpest bolt could not penetrate the giant's body.

She tried to swallow down her terror as the giant pulverized the mountainside with each step he took behind them. *What does he want with us? To what end does this monster force us up the mountain?* She'd read nothing of rock giants in the *Grimoire*, though she shivered in remembrance of a tune Granda sometimes sang:

> *'Twas high in the mountains when she 'eard them rumble,*
> *When the peaks did crumble, and stumble nigh.*

The creature grunted to prod them along and they hurried as best they could, but the trail roughened, flanked by jutting walls that caught on cloth and skin. Only the giant traversed effortlessly over the terrain.

They climbed for hours without reprieve under a murky sky. Wynn slipped and fell more than once, covering his cloak in silt and scraping his bound hands raw. Lia's body screamed in revolt. When she could push no farther, she halted and cried out, "Please, we need to rest."

The giant stopped and stood guard over them like a crudely chiseled statue. Lia held her eyes on their captor while she eased herself onto a perch. Wynn nudged himself beside her.

"Here, drink this," was all she dared to utter. She helped Wynn with her water skin and then used the edge of her cloak to wipe the sweat and dust from his face. Only their eyes spoke encouragement to one another. The giant watched expressionless, but as soon as they finished, he grumbled to move them along.

The trail snaked around the vast boulders, but the giant prodded them to climb straight up the rocks. Wynn slid and fell in his efforts to scale the knife-edged stones. "Ruddy spades!"

The giant swooped down his hand and scooped Wynn up like a sack of flour, tossing him over his shoulders. Lia gasped. "No! Let him go!"

A cold grunt and her cousin's agonized moans assaulted Lia, and she knew there was nothing to do but keep moving. She winced at the horses' screams, and watched the giant lift the animals, one in each hand, over the bone-breaking terrain. She could only wonder at his motive for keeping their animals safe.

Lia lumbered onward and weariness met with exasperation when the steepness of the mountain forced to her to climb on all fours. Through silt-filled tears, she saw the scarlet rivers on her torn hands. Every moment of climbing over the rocks drew more from her flesh and still the giant pushed her onward.

The day dragged across the sky and the dimly lit sun melted into the horizon. Lia's body trembled in hunger and exhaustion, and Wynn groaned in pain from the ceaseless jostling. The mountain crest called to Lia and she pushed with every fiber to put an end to her climb.

In a rush of relief, she reached the top and dizzily scanned the view. The Sea of Morgandy stretched across the western horizon, dying rays of gold scattered across silver blue. She knew that somewhere near its edge dwelt the *Great Nion*. The empty flat and fae forest reached out to the south, and to the north, continued a vast array of snow-covered mountains poking at the sky. The east lay hidden, shrouded behind a wall of fog.

The giant dumped Wynn in a crumpled heap onto the ground, and then tore up several scraggy bushes. He lit them afire with a snap of his flint-stone fingers. Lia drew back at the spark he created, and gasped when he yanked the saddlebags off the horses and tossed them toward her. She stared quizzically at the creature while she pulled the bags close.

The rock giant loosened his hold on the horses and the animals lowered their noses. A stream of water trickled along a crack in the soil, just enough to satiate their thirst.

Lia bent down to Wynn and helped him sit upright. "You all right?"

He grimaced. "My back, arms . . . I'll live."

"For whatever reason, he's keeping us alive," Lia murmured. She rummaged through the saddlebags, pausing briefly to run her fingers over the heart etching. "Come back in one piece," Kelven had said.

She withdrew her knapsack, thankful to have stuffed it within the saddlebags, along with a filled skin delicately stitched with a pattern of eternity spirals and interlaced love knots. It was Da's favorite traveling skin.

She poured a measure of mead from the skin onto each of her hands, biting down on her lip as the fermented honey stung her wounds. Then she turned to Wynn. "Here, drink some," she said, fitting the skin between his palms.

She pulled at his wrist bindings, the strange vines loosening to her touch, but then wrapping back tight when she let go. Intrigued, she repeated her touch and release, and the vines responded the same way. "They must be enchanted."

"Thanks anyway," Wynn muttered and swigged on the mead.

Lia heated a cluster of *Luis* berries on the fire while the giant stared down at them from his post, unmoving and silent. For now, Lia tried to ignore his presence. She stuffed the cooked berries into a chunk of bread and replaced the skin in Wynn's hands with the food.

"That mead and these berries'll give you a boost. Put your back to the fire, the heat'll help."

Wynn eyed the orange-red mash, and Lia added, "The berries have to be cooked first—changes the seed inside so you don't get sick."

"As if my innards could get any more wrecked," he said, nudging closer to the fire.

Lia made a quick pottage, boiling a few carrots and spring onions with a hunk of salt pork. Nothing fancy, but the food tasted like bliss.

She cleaned their bowls and packed everything back up. "I think the best we can do is rest. Looks like he'll be watching us all night," she whispered.

Wynn nodded with heavy eyes. "I'll sleep now, thanks to that mead. It's like gold in my veins."

"That's what Da always called it, 'liquid gold'." Lia pushed back her tears.

The giant's gaze etched into her back and she eased away from her cousin. The rock giant showed no interest in their food, nor did he sit down to rest. Lia pondered on the formation of such a creature. *Magic*, she thought. Only pure, powerful magic could transform a pile of stones into such animation. So, who wielded such power, and what fate did this magician have in store for them?

With her bedroll left behind in the mountainside alcove, Lia pulled her cloak tightly about her. Her hair served as a makeshift scarf across her mouth and chin, and the lasting scent of her mother's soap brought her comfort. She tossed and turned half the night, shifting her eyes from the giant to the fire's hypnotic flames, until sleep overcame her.

Sinister laughter rings in her ears while the fog presses down. No! Not again! *All at once, tendrils creep up her legs, wrapping and binding them. Long barbs pierce into her skin and she cries in agony. But the pain on her flesh is nothing compared to the waves of sorrow, waves of wretched torment, flooding through her soul.* Make it stop! Please! *Then something burns on her chest. She claws at the pouch aflame from the light within.*

"Glrk! Sheeok!"

Lia awoke with a start. The looming creature motioned for her to rise, and she lifted her sore body with the nightmare still pounding in her head. Not a nightmare, she reminded herself, but an undeniable fate-dream. Since the night before they left for Brume, a force had seized her dreams. This fate-dream hovered over her now like a roc—a giant vulture circling in wait—and the *Straif* verse rattled from her memory:

Beware jagged pricks from this arrow of the mist.

Wynn's face hung and he grimaced as he stood. Only the horses seemed eager to move, perhaps smelling better pastures nearby. Their fate eluded Lia, so a mix of relief and wariness swept through her when the giant prodded them west toward the *Nion.* The Sea of Morgandy shone like a beacon under the periwinkle sky, and every step they took drew them closer to a cure for the *Straif's* poison. Lia could only wonder if they'd make it that far.

The mountaintop's landscape flattened and vegetation thickened along a swelling stream. The weather and surroundings seemed almost fae-like as they continued across the plateau. Golden-red roe deer frolicked across the grasses, jackrabbits and hedgehogs scampered by, and flocks of birds glided arrow-like across the sky. Lia eyed the thickening evergreens, a perfect place for her to flee, but where would that leave Wynn and the horses?

The rock giant trudged close behind them, smashing anything underfoot—bushes, small trees, and a few ill-fated rodents. With every step he made, dust and gravel tumbled from his body. Lia kept her feet ever swift in case he mistook her for a common shrub.

They crested a small incline and Lia gasped. "Look, there!"

In the distance, where the cliffs and sea joined, stood a solitary tree. The biggest tree she had ever seen. She reasoned they were too close to trek in any other direction now. *Perhaps the giant is helping us after all.* He forced them to move at an exhausting pace, but he never truly harmed them. He carried the horses when they would've fallen, and he was leading them to their desired destination.

"I don't like it," Wynn grumbled, staring at the *Nion*. "Why'd we need the bumbling escort?"

Lia understood his trepidation, but all of her unease faded as she fixed her eyes on the tree. The silhouette of the *Nion* tree pressed against the sky and against her mind. The tension in her body sifted away, and her thoughts wrapped like garlands around the tree.

"Watch out!" Wynn shouted.

Lia paused in her step. An ebony snake slid across her boots. It raised its head and peered at her with ruby eyes before it moved up the path before them in silence. The giant seemed unimpressed and grunted loudly, moving them along.

The snake never ventured too far ahead and even stopped when they did at a stream. The horses drank in endless gulps, like camels after a long trek. Wynn sat on a rock with his brow drawn together while Lia retrieved her water skin and a slab of jerky, nearly dropping both. Her mind floated like feathers amid the landscape, leaving all other thoughts behind.

"What's with you?" Wynn said under his breath.

Lia turned from him, disquieted by his question, and sighed before the cool waters. Her cloak fell to the ground and she bent languidly down to the stream. *That's better.* She gazed into the clear pool and splashed the dust off her travel-worn face. As she smoothed her red tresses, her reflection in the waters changed. The woman looking back was older and weeping, and she looked remarkably like Ma.

A chill ran up Lia's spine and her mind cleared from its strange fog. "Grandma Myrna?"

Grandma nodded beneath the watery mirror.

"Grf! Urzak!" The giant's voice boomed, almost knocking Lia over.

Grandma's image washed away, and Lia cried out, "Wait!" But the giant motioned her from the stream and back onto the trail.

Wynn peered at her. "What is going on, Lee? You act like you're sleepwalking."

"I don't know," she murmured, and then her gaze latched on the *Nion* once more.

Wynn's voice turned to muffled whispers across Lia's ears. She no longer cared what he might be saying. Nothing mattered but the tree—the glorious, inviting tree that became grander with each step closer. Every moment Lia looked on its crown, her whole being flooded with hypnotic bliss.

Something of such beauty could never harbor anything unpleasant . . .

The giant allowed for no further rest and even pushed them to a faster pace. Lia was pleased. On and on they marched until land met sea. Waves crashed below the cliffs and the salt air brushed across her face.

The *Great Nion* set upon a large knoll with its arms opened to a coral sky. It wore a full yet airy canopy. Its feathery leaves danced in the breeze, all flanked by sooty black buds freckling its numerous branches. Lia recognized this tree. She knew its glory like the palm of her hand, for its very image emblazoned the front cover of Grandma's *Grimoire*.

The black snake reappeared, lifted its head, and moved toward the tree. Lia followed it.

"Lee, no!" Wynn leapt toward her. The giant's fist came down with a thunk in front of him. Merrie let out a high-pitched neigh and Nolan snorted. They both pulled against their leads. The giant tossed away their lead ropes as if his job suddenly ended with the beasts.

Lia barely took notice. Her thoughts spun with the *Nion*. "I have to go on, Wynn. It's why we've come." She chased after the snake, reeling toward the tree, giving in to its magnetic pull.

She crested the grassy knoll and halted. The *Nion* filled her senses and she swooned. Her eyes barely held the span of its trunk, and her lungs drew in its rich scent. A maze of vertical ridges, deep enough for Lia to stand in, rippled down gray bark to the base of the tree. Her eyes flickered over the exposed roots, and then her breath caught when she spotted a steaming cauldron.

Rootbound

The snake maneuvered through the roots of the *Nion* tree and disappeared into an underground lair. Lia crept closer and noticed a ditch of red-hot flames under the boiling cauldron. The pot gleamed with silver etchings she took for ancient writings.

A breeze tugged at her cloak and a tinkle of chimes resounded. Movement from a deep ridge in the *Nion* caught Lia's eye. One by one, three shrouded figures appeared, like the three outlined figures on the cover of Grandma's *Grimoire*. Lia's heart skipped in anticipation, but the mysterious trio aimed their focus on the cauldron.

Like the screech of a tormented animal, the eldritch voice of the figure in black cried out, "Root of mandragora torn from the soil, after the scream and while the water boils."

A boney, bloodless hand threw a tuberous root into the brew. Lia recognized the toxic mandrake by its human-shaped root. Snowy webs of hair escaped from beneath the figure's hood and Lia's breath caught when the ancient crone turned toward her.

Just then the second figure spoke, her voice a tranquil stream, "Deadly nightshade enters our greal, we'll fly all night, over hill and dale." A feminine hand tossed in a branch covered with midnight berries. She turned toward Lia, pushing back her crimson hood to reveal a face etched in beauty and framed in waves of black velvet.

The third, smaller figure approached the cauldron, surrounded by a menagerie. Butterflies and bees danced around her head, marmots and bunnies snuggled at her feet, and her voice sang out like a bird's, "Henn-belle let us hear you ring, we welcome all prophecies that you bring."

She dropped clusters of yellow, funnel-shaped flowers veined in deep purple into the boiling abyss. Gold-spun tresses tumbled from her hood, and the girl exposed her cherub face.

Lia drew closer, careful to remain far enough from the noxious miasma wafting from the brew. Even with its poisons, she was enthralled by the conjured magic.

"I'm Lia Griene from the village of Rock—"

"We know who ye are, child, and why yer here. 'Tis why we sent ye Jokur the giant, a right worthy guide," the crone crackled through thin, bleached lips. If the odious voice was any indication of the woman's appearance, Lia was glad her hood remained covering her head.

The girl giggled. "I told him to bring your horses. They're such lovely creatures."

The ancient woman snorted at her, and rattled on, "Ye favor yer grandam's looks, hair like a scorched sky, but ye've a lot more fire. Pity she shied from us, we coulda' saved her."

Saved her?" Lia said.

"Saved her life! 'Twas shameful how she sacrificed her gifts, her very soul."

"No . . . she died at home, Granda said the dropsy took her—"

"Dropsy, is it?" The crone let out a mirthless cackle, its shrill jabbing daggers against Lia's skull. Then her voice turned strident. "Guess he didn't know what else it could be, eh? Sucked dry by a bunch of shades she was, her soul doomed to this forbidden land forever. Nothing but a slave-wraith now."

Lia's head swam and her knees went weak. "Slave wraith? No, they had a pact . . . the shades . . . she brought them food, she wielded the amber."

"Clever tricksters! They tasted her bread, imbibed her ale, devoured her soul."

Lia's stomach lurched, the taste of bile on her tongue.

"Do not fret the past." A honeyed voice poured into Lia's ears, instantly soothing her troubled mind. She stared at the raven-haired woman with skin like fresh cream and eyes of liquid lapis. "All that ever matters is the present, this very moment. Look at where you are. You are the one, Lia Griene, gifted far beyond your people, far beyond your grandmother."

"No," Lia said, uneasy with being esteemed above Grandma Myrna. "Her wisdom, skills, she—"

"—chose her fate," the woman cooed. "She used the shades and their vile master as much as they used her. Theirs was a long friendship, built around her yearning for this land and their insatiable greed. They gave her passage into Brume—her true home—and in return, she fed them the magic of her soul."

Lia shuddered in memory of the shades. "Is her soul truly bound to them, doomed forever?"

"Forever is a long time, my dear, just ask the *Idho* tree. As I said, all that ever really matters is now, the present. So, what do you wish for at this moment?" The woman peered into Lia's eyes.

"I . . . we need medicine, a cure to save my da, Granda, the others—" her words grew thick on her tongue.

"Hm-hmm and why not figure out this elixir on your own? You underestimate your abilities, Lia." Her melodious voice circled around Lia's head. "You know the roots, the trees, the flowers, and the bees. You feel the earth, and run with the wind. You know the soil, she's a loyal friend."

Lia's head filled with the woman's sing-song words, her body swaying to its melody. Her feet sank down, rooting within the rich soil, setting firm within the earth's grasp. She didn't try to move away, didn't want to. The solid hold gave her comfort. It was as if she was a fellow tree, setting roots to mingle with the *Nion's*.

The woman's voice poured thick into Lia's mind and she swam in its euphoria. She longed for the woman's praise, needed to prove to all three tree guardians the depth of her skills. "I'd, um, start with some leaves and bark from this sacred *Nion* tree."

"First part solved. So clever you are. Only twelve parts more to decipher. Listen carefully, for I will recite this only once: There's three parts herb, and two parts tree, a snippet of golden bough, and a bit of the enemy; combine with sacred alicorn, under the light of a sentry stone, brewed in the blood of Brume, by maiden, mother, and crone."

Lia listened intently, running the spell through her head, the potion echoing surprisingly clear. Thirteen parts in total, and she knew three of the ingredients right away: *Nion* tree, golden bough, and the enemy—the menacing *Straif*.

"Tsk-tsk," the woman clicked her tongue and waved her finger at Lia. "You're fretting again. Mustn't lose focus. Don't let that old bramble intimidate you. A bit of Brume's blood'll do the trick."

"Oh, stop coddling her! Enough of this nonsense." The crone slathered a frothy green salve along the tangled roots of the tree.

A hawk cried out before it landed on a high branch. Its cry jolted Lia from her trance, and she noticed the horses grazing in the distance. Near them, the giant towered over Wynn while he balanced on the precipice of the cliff.

"Wynn!" She tried to take a step, but her feet remained planted to the ground.

"Ahh, let him be, Jokur will tend to him." The woman's voice flowed back into Lia's head like syrup.

Lia's mind screamed for Wynn, but webs spun within her, tightly cocooning her mind until she was deep in the woman's spell once again.

"We bore that rock giant from the crags of these mountains, something you could learn to do in time," the woman said. "Now, back to your task at hand, dear girl. Show me how you've mastered your craft."

Lia gazed at the woman, eager once more to hear her soothing voice, to prove her skills. Herblore, treelore, legends of old, these things shone clear in her mind. In fact, she'd never been so sharp in her knowledge of them. Wynn became a blurred thought, a vague memory from another place and time. All that mattered was the *Nion* tree, its guardians, and figuring out the elixir. However, the importance of the elixir began to elude her.

It must be to prove my ability. Yes, that's it.

"Dandelion is quite purifying and so is cleavers," Lia said.

The woman smiled. "Yes, lion's tooth and grass of goose will work just fine."

The girl reached up and broke off a small branch from the tree. She skipped forward and handed it to Lia. "Take this piece of the *Nion*. It's been kissed by honeydew."

94

Lia grasped the branch sprinkled with droplets of dew. They shone like tears of sunshine against the delicate leaves and smooth bark.

"But nothing is sweeter than *Saille* tree honey. Bzzzzz!" The girl twirled herself around, flapping her arms under her cloak. "You'll need her bark for your potion, too." She buzzed in a whirl and plopped on the ground. Her high-pitched giggle spilled forth as a squirrel careened over the roots and disappeared up the trunk.

Lia breathed the girl in like a springtime breeze. The fae-like terrain and the countless animals flocking near were touched by the enchantments of the *Nion's* youngest guardian. By her wishes, the giant had brought Merrie and Nolan along safely.

Watching the girl, Lia longed for her own childhood. She spent hours making pies in the mud, climbing maples in the Bryns, watching the birds and insects. After washing and mending one too many linen kirtles, Ma had finally given in to Lia's boyish ways, and allowed her to wear sturdy breeches and boots from then on.

"Ma," Lia whispered. Images of her mother washed through her mind, pressing against the dreamy fog.

"Oh, bloody bells! Ye've appeased her enough with all that 'lixir talk, got her head plenty deep in the clouds, her feet good and rooted with the *Nion*." The crone threw a gnarled root into the cauldron. "But our brew's 'bout cooked and the boy's in place. Time to end these games and get on with her rites."

Lia's gut flinched and her muscles tensed. The scratchy voice of the crone tore the webs in her head. "Rites? Boy's in place?"

The crone cackled. "'Tis why yer here, lass, so we's can bind ye, and the boy's life'll make a right fine sacrifice."

"No!" Euphoria battled with the horror of their plan. She shook her head, trying to free herself from the woman's spell, and nearly tumbled over dizzy.

"Hush now, hag." The beautiful woman's voice missed its honeyed sound. "Lia child, you are one of us; we knew you the second you stepped foot into Brume. Special magic runs in your blood, passed down from your grandmother. An extraordinary power she claimed with her very first breath, her first seconds of life, drawn from the enchanted fog. She perished from her own desperate need, but now you've come, so much stronger—"

"Enough!" Lia threw up her hands like a wall. With a strength of will she'd never known, she pushed away the woman's power. The final vestiges of the spell unraveled, and Lia's thoughts broke free. However, the truths about Grandma Myrna remained engraved on her mind.

The woman's lips clamped shut and a troubled expression marred her exquisite face. All three guardians appeared transfixed, as if carefully weighing their options.

Lia's feet remained tied, entwined within the roots of the tree. She inhaled its pungent scent, felt the beating of its pulse vibrating in her soul. A sudden wash of energy poured through her, the sacred *Nion* offering a glimpse of its mystery, a taste of its magic.

It promised her unbounded power and immortality, an existence rooted in earth's wisdom, eternally nurtured by sea and sky, a blissful life without end. But, it came at too high a price. Her body, her soul, would meld with the tree, her entire being forever merged within its embrace. Wynn's life, the memory of home and family, Kelven, all would be lost to her as she became bound to the *Great Nion*.

Lia smiled at the young girl now plaiting her sun-kissed hair. She reminded her of the undine faery preening her locks in the soapsuds. And the memory sparked an idea. "I have a gift for you, something very special."

"What nonsense is this?" the crone shrieked, wringing her skeletal hands.

"Ooooh! I love gifts." The young girl clapped her hands.

"It's in my bag, on my horse. Shall I whistle for her?" Lia slowly turned her feet and realized the *Nion* tree had already honored her choice and set her free.

"Yes, yes! Bring your mare," the girl squealed.

The raven-haired woman stood mute, her face etched in anger.

Merrie perked up to the sound of Lia's whistle, as if waking from a deep slumber. She shook her mane and trotted toward her mistress. Nolan didn't seem to notice, his muzzle hanging in a stupor. Jokur and Wynn stood at the cliff's edge, waiting. Wynn's face was turned toward the *Nion*, but Lia knew the grassy knoll and tree branches obscured his view of her. *Hold on, Wynn, just a little longer!*

Merrie nuzzled Lia with her velveteen nose. Lia breathed in the horse's familiar smell, the musk filling her with memories of home, of Da. She opened her bag and brought out a brick imbued with golden swirls and the scent of elf leaf. Then she witnessed a rare scene. All three guardians, steeped in ancient magic, appeared baffled.

"What do we need with some pretty block of . . . stone?" The crone's voice had weakened.

The girl stared at it wide-eyed. "'Tis too dark for citrine, and look at all those swirls. Oh please, what is it?"

The woman remained quiet, her eyes turned to a dark sea. The air chilled, a salty breeze stirred, and time ran thin. Lia had silenced the woman's voice, had paused her next move, but unlike the *Nion* tree, the woman would not part with Lia so easily.

"This comes from a magnificent recipe my ma created. It's truly a wonder." Lia leapt toward the cauldron, holding her breath against the fumes, and threw the block of soap into the brew. Within seconds, a mass of foam formed and bubbles spewed over the edges of the pot.

"Grab the ladle!" the crone rattled.

"Oh no, oh no, oh no!" The young girl jumped up and down.

Lia quickly mounted Merrie while the woman stood with her arms raised to the skies.

Jokur and Wynn aimed their attention skyward at the massive black clouds converging overhead. The winds gusted forth, claps of thunder banged, and Lia struggled to keep steady. She swung around her crossbow and set a bolt in place on the stock. She kicked Merrie into a charging gallop and kept her eyes on the giant. Jokur took notice of the charging pair, exposing the target. Her aim was true, the sharp bolt landing firmly within the black depths of one eye.

A deafening rumble poured out of the rock giant's mouth. He threw Wynn's sword aside and grabbed at the black ooze on his face. Stumbling blindly, he teetered on the cliff's edge, his feet struggling for purchase until he fell into the abyss below. Lia closed her eyes against the cloud of debris stirred by the deluge of crashing rocks.

When the dust dissipated in a downpour of rain, she realized Wynn had vanished too.

Waterlogged

ooo!" Lia's voice echoed across the waters below. She jumped off Merrie and flew to the precipice, peering downward into the wall of fog. From the depths of mist, a pair of hands emerged followed by a clump of yellow hair. Lia let out a sigh of relief, and helped pull Wynn up over the edge.

"Just some . . . weakling girl . . . huh? Let 'em all . . . see you now," he rasped.

Lia gripped under his shoulder, taking note of the new gashes across his arms and spots of blood soaking through his tunic. "Are you all right? Can you ride?"

"Yeah." He coughed, leaning against her. "Good thing those bindings fell from my wrists, all of a sudden too, like vines shriveling in the sun." Nolan ambled close, snorting, and Wynn struggled to mount him. "Horse was in some kind of daze. Guess all the racket woke him up."

Lia scurried off and returned with his blade. "You'll be wanting this back."

The winds died as quickly as they had been conjured, and the horses cantered from the edge of the cliff. Lia tried to veer her eyes from the *Nion* tree, to muffle the echo of the crone's cackle, and to ignore the silence of the spellbinding woman. But she was compelled to see it one more time before they fled. She ventured a glance toward the base of the *Nion* and found the cauldron sitting cold and the guardians missing from their posts. They had gone back into the tree, defeated.

The thirteen-part elixir spun through Lia's mind, and a mix of hope and dread filled her. For now, she kept the newfound quest to herself. Wynn needed his wounds cleaned and a good night's sleep before hearing they weren't headed home.

They galloped their horses as fast as Wynn's battered body could stand, slowing down only when the *Nion* became a silhouette behind them. They progressed across the plateau in search of a place to camp. The terrain grew unfamiliar and the clouds thickened in the twilight sky, spitting down just enough rain to hinder their sight.

"There, just ahead," Lia said, catching sight of a dense grove. A swollen brook meandered through a thicket of *Fearn* trees, and they found a secluded place near the water's edge. Lia breathed easier within the copse, its canopy of green providing a welcome roof.

Wynn groaned as he slid off his horse, and Lia bade him sit still while she set up camp. The trees clustered together in a shelter of umber-brown trunks and dangling catkins. She collected pieces of the alder wood for kindling, the white inner bark turning blood red with each cut from her knife. Then she heard the flutes.

She jerked her head around, but Wynn seemed undisturbed. Her hand tingled against the *Fearn* wood, and a subtle sensation trickled up her arm. A breeze wafted through the grove and more soft tones danced on the air.

Pandean pipes, she thought. The melody danced through the shield of trees like a chorus to the running stream. Lia scanned the grove and a hundred pair of eyes peered back at her.

Ohhh. "Are you fae," she whispered, hoping they were friendly, "like those in the meadow? Or maybe tree sprites?"

"What?" Wynn grumbled.

"We're not alone."

Wynn moved for his sword.

"It's all right, Wynn. It's nothing like that," she said. "They're fae of some sort."

The tingling in Lia's body intensified and somehow she knew the energy of the trees ran through her. It was similar to her connection with the *Nion*, though the *Fearns* exuded their own essence. A stronger sense of the shy creatures filled her. Their playfulness permeated her mind and she relaxed.

As if she had newly grown antennae, Lia reached out with her thoughts and probed into one of the trees. She didn't know who was more startled, she or the tree sprites, when she barged into their realm. A frenzy of whispers chattered through her mind while the sprites scrambled about.

I'm in the tree. My thoughts, my mind's eye is here with the fae! Like mindspeak, only better. Stronger.

"Friendly, er, greetings," Lia imparted.

She heard more whispers, several giggles, and a few hiccups. Waves of auburn hair and honeyed skin washed through Lia's mind, and she sensed the sprites' devotion for the *Fearns*.

She focused her thoughts on the sprites, trying to use her mind's eye to capture sight of one. Rather than flitting about like the *geancanach* in the meadow, the *Fearn* tree faeries melded in and out of the rich surrounding wood. Lia focused on one spot within the tree, and her breath caught when a sprite came into view.

Verdant eyes shone from the faery's bronze face. Soft moss covered the length of her torso, and long reddish-brown hair cascaded down to her waist. She tilted her head and smiled.

Lia gasped as a sudden force yanked her away from the fae and pulled her downward, down the tree's trunk, down, down, until her mind's eye plunged into the stream. She anchored her mind against the *Fearn*'s sturdy roots and tried to reclaim her wits.

A woman's voice permeated the waters, and though she didn't understand how, Lia recognized it. "Listen, child. Find me at the headless *Eadha*, where the black waters roil."

"Grandma!" Lia shot out her thoughts in every direction, but only the stream's gentle gurgling answered her cry. "Please, where are you? Come back. Talk to me!"

"Lee," Wynn's voice cut through all other sound.

Lia's mind shot out of the waters, out of the *Fearn* tree, and back to where she sat near her frantic cousin. "Wynn."

"What in spades is going on? It's like you weren't here! Your eyes were all glazed over, and when I called out your name, you just stared, like you couldn't hear me at all."

Lia blinked at him. His brow was creased in panic and a few gashes still gleamed from his fall. She pushed her disquiet aside. Now was not the time to alarm Wynn about Grandma. "I'm all right. Everything's fine. I just got a little . . . fae-struck is all. I'll make up a fire and we can both get some food and rest."

She shifted her focus to her tasks, and soon had an array of pots simmering over the fire. She concocted a quick wound salve, mumbling out the names of the herbs.

"Did you just say *burr burr*?" Wynn asked, eyes heavy.

Lia stifled a smile. "I wondered myself about the old names. I mean, who came up with cuckoo's bread for plantain leaves or bloody butcher for valerian root?"

He gave her a sideways grin and Lia pushed a steamy mug into his hand. "Here, drink some bear's foot while I get your soup."

Wynn held his bruised side as he chuckled.

Lia breathed relief when her cousin dozed off. He barely got his food down before he was snoring. Now, the healing powers of sleep claimed his body. He'd need all the strength he could gain for their journey ahead.

The herbs Ebrill had her gather from the meadow wouldn't cure Granda or Da, but they were more powerful than any back home. It would buy them time, Lia assured herself. Time they all desperately needed.

The firelight grew soft and the stream trickled a lullaby through the naked tree roots, but Lia couldn't sleep. The last few days whirled inside her head. She'd seen and heard too much to sort it all out at once. The thirteen-part elixir ran like mud through her mind. Half of the pieces remained unsolved and one part meant contending with the *Straif.*

Grandma Myrna presented another quest. The words of the *Nion* guardian echoed in Lia's head, "Sacrificed 'er very soul," and, "Slave-wraith." The crone said the shades and their master had stolen Grandma's life and taken her magic. *How? And who was this master?*

Lia recalled the haunting verse from the *Grimoire:*

> For the call of magic, I do what I must;
> Sacrifice is needed to do what is just.
> The dark master beckons, and his command I do heed;
> Anything I will do for flower, root, and seed.
> And after my life does perish,
> And the magic fades toward its end,
> I know the children will come forth and bring it back again.

Grandma's spirit had reached out from Brume's waters and summoned Lia to an *Eadha* tree. But what could a headless tree have

105

to do with Grandma's soul? And what had the *Nion* woman meant when she said, "Her very first breath, her first seconds of life, drawn from the enchanted fog"?

Lia struggled to get her mind around all the revelations. Baffled beyond thought, she reached up and grabbed the pouch hanging against her chest. She dropped the crystal into her palm and it cast a spray of rainbows against the firelight. Its prism faces led to several hexagonal points, and like magic wands, the crowns exuded a strange heat in her hand.

"Another mystery," she whispered.

Frustrated and exhausted, she nestled close to the fire and ran her fingers through her hair like Ma used to do until she fell asleep. A dream danced through her head of a royal procession, colored in purples, reds, and gold. A fair-haired king marched at its head, followed by his court. In keeping faith with the people, they emanated everything royalty should be, and nothing like the heartless rulers of Nemetona.

Lia awoke before dawn and left Wynn to his slumbers while she searched for a way back down to the valley. The grove spanned along the mountain's edge, shielding her from the world beyond it. After several attempts down different trailheads, she came upon one with ample breadth and smooth ground. Satisfied, she sped back to camp.

"Wynn, time to wake." Lia nudged him.

"Wha . . . what time is it?" He rubbed his eyes.

"Sunrise. How do you feel?"

"Sore. Thirsty. I'll live." He rose from his spot and knelt at the edge of the brook, splashing cold water onto his face.

Lia packed up their things and set Wynn out a hunk of bread with a slab of cheese.

"Your salve helped, and that bear's foot really *kicked* me to sleep." A half-hearted smile tugged at his lips. He scooped up his fare and mounted Nolan.

Lia smiled back, though her nerves fluttered in her stomach. "I found a trail earlier this morning. Should take us back down into the valley where we can head . . . east."

"East?" Wynn coughed, spewing breadcrumbs. "But, that's where that deadly tree is."

Lia swallowed hard. "Yes, I know."

Wynn veered Nolan closer to Lia. "All right, I've had my rest, now it's time to talk. I thought the remedy was at the *Nion*, that you'd found it and we might be heading back now. What in billhooks happened back there anyway?"

Lia took a deep breath. "I know you couldn't see them, but there were guardians, keepers of the tree: an old crone, a girl, and the most beautiful woman. The woman's magic was powerful, hypnotic. The three of them brewed a binding potion, a spell to keep me there, and you, well, you were to be the blood sacrifice."

Wynn scowled. "Ma was right, this trickster land devours people."

Lia's ma had said much the same: "Brume has an insatiable

appetite. Your grandma lost a piece of herself every time she ventured there."

"All right, what else?" Wynn said.

Lia eyed him warily. "The *Nion* tree started to, well, merge with me somehow."

His brow pinched. "Merge?"

"I know it sounds strange, but it was quite amazing." She paused, remembering the tree's power. "Anyway, the woman also gave me the cure, or at least a recipe for the elixir. It's in spell form, a riddle to be deciphered, and a piece from the *Straif* is one part of it—"

"Oh, ruddy spades!" Wynn's eyes flashed blue fire and Nolan snorted at his master's distress. "This place is nothing *but* riddles, each one more deadly than the last. And now you're telling me we have to go tangle with that menacing *bramble?*" His voice tore through the grove, every muscle in his face contorting with anger.

"It's the only way!" Hot tears sprung from Lia's eyes. She knew Wynn had suffered, had a right to be angry, but his words chipped at her resolve and the burden of their plight pressed hard upon her shoulders.

He dragged his hand across his glowering face and pulled his cloak tight. "Fine. East it is then."

Lia nudged Merrie into a walk and they set off down the mountain trail. A drizzle of rain began to fall, matching Lia's mood. Her hair matted against her face and her mind drowned in worry. *Wynn's right. Nothing about this land has been straightforward.* Like the twisting of a vine, a new quest came up at every turn. From Ebrill's ominous words, "The dark power grows stronger as the enchantment weakens," to the *Luis* tree wyrm's warning, "The guardians are losing power. Darkness devours the veil," and all the other mysteries she'd pondered during the night, their journey entangled them deeper within its grasp.

After a long and silent ride, Wynn called out, "There, to the left. Let's stop for a bit."

Lia turned Merrie into a sheltered inlet. They dismounted their horses and Wynn offered Lia his water skin. "You found a decent trail."

Lia silently agreed. Sprigs of plant life jutted out of every stone fissure, blanketing the path in green. It was plenty wide for the horses, and the gradual, easterly decline made for an easy ride headed in the right direction.

They sat upon a flat stone, and Wynn said, "Lee, I know two things real well: farming and sword fighting, neither of which seem to do much good here. I know we have no choice, so how about telling me more about this elixir."

Lia wiped her mouth and handed back his water skin. "It has thirteen parts. Three are herbs, of which I know two for sure. Two are trees, and I know them both. Another part is golden bough, and another part is the enemy—the *Straif*. Then it gets confusing." Wynn's brow started to furrow. "It calls for alicorn, which I haven't figured out yet. By the light of a sentry stone—don't know this either—brewed in the blood of Brume by a mother, a maiden, and a crone."

Wynn sighed before an impish smirk crossed his lips. "I know one. You, you're the blushing maiden."

Lia opened her mouth and smacked his arm. Then she realized he had a point. She drew up her leather pouch and released her stone, handing it to Wynn. "I've been wondering more about this, too. The quartz grows warm in my hand, and in my dreams it burns into a blaze of light."

"Hmm, I don't feel anything." He placed the crystal back into her hand. "Grandma figured out how to wield the amber. Maybe it's your turn with that stone. Maybe you've found your own talisman."

Lia beamed at his insight. A talisman, rooted from her garden by her loyal hound. "Well, there's a verse in the *Grimoire* that reads,"

There is an art to the gathering of stones,
A respect and care in retrieving earth's bones—

"No more riddles!" Wynn put his hands over his ears before he turned serious. "Listen, it's been four days since we left Granda and Kelven, and I can only hope they've made it back all right. If we hurry, we should make the valley floor by dusk."

Of course they returned safe, Lia assured herself. If anyone could get Granda home in one piece, it was Kelven. Tending to her granda, cajoling a horse, plunging through haunted fog, none of it seemed too much for Kelven to manage. Then a woeful pang shot through Lia at the thought of Ma's reaction when Kelven arrived with Granda ailing and news that Lia and Wynn were still in Brume. And all while she tended to Da.

Da, Lia thought, and she swallowed down her tears. It'd been a sennight—one full week—since the day of his attack. Ebrill had told her that the meadow's herbs would cool the poison-induced fever and diminish the pain. They were the best magic she could offer and Lia was grateful. Everyday the herbs added to Da and Granda's lives was another day closer to the cure. *The Straif's poison will not win. We will find what is needed and defeat this bane!*

"Let's get moving." Lia mounted Merrie and continued down the trail.

The rain subsided as the curtain of gray tore into shreds, and the first eager star winked its greeting. They drove the horses down the mountain in silence and by dusk's sherbet glow, Lia made out the terrain below. A tiny groan slid from her mouth.

Her eyes roved over the bog sprawling across the valley floor. Numerous streams wound their way around islands of peat moss, and Lia questioned how the horses would traverse it. To the south, the bog edged the fae grove; to the west, stretched the barren flat; and to the east, a forest stood like a wall of green backed by a foggy horizon.

"Hopefully, we can skirt the base of this mountain," Wynn said. "The horses'll get stuck walking through this fen."

When the trail ended, it was difficult to find dry ground. Merrie reared her head and neighed, her feet plunging in and out of the muck. Nolan fared a little better with his greater height and friskier nature.

"I see a place ahead where we can camp," Wynn called out, leading the way.

They tucked themselves into the cove before the final arrows of daylight vanished. There was enough scraggy brush growing through the rocks to build up a small fire, and though it didn't give off much heat, Lia was able to boil water for a quick soup.

They finished every drop of the meal, and Lia exchanged the pot for the kettle. "That was the last of the salt pork and we've only a handful of vegetables left. We can use the remaining cheese and fruit tomorrow; then we'll have to scavenge." She rummaged through her knapsack. "But, I've herbs. I can make you any kind of tea you want and I've just enough honey to sweeten two more mugs."

"I don't think I'll need any more foot-of-bear. You wouldn't happen to have something called maiden's magnet or maybe greatest swordsman?" Wynn asked wryly.

"For you I have just the thing," Lia said. "How about a nice decoction of ass's foot?"

Wynn gave her a half smile and stretched close to the fire. "All right, you got me there." With a yawn, he tightened his cloak, and was soon asleep.

Lia brushed the day's travel from her hair until her scalp tingled and sparks flew from the long tresses. She leaned against the mountainside and scanned the peat bog shimmering under the starry sky, wondering at the vastness of Brume. Three of its borders with

Nemetona were clear: Dunley Meadow, the Sea of Morgandy, and the Bryns. But what of the northern region? What lay in and beyond the icy mountains?

She peered into the fire, the flames licking at the shadows, and she drifted to sleep.

Thorny stalks slither up a charred stump, plunging into the dark waters that fill it. The Straif! *Deeper and deeper the pythonic stems snake in, tunneling through deadened roots to their well-worn path. Numerous tendrils poke up through the hillside soil, bright sunlight shining on their razor spines.* It seeks! *Green hills stretch below, speckled with crystal towers.* In Rockberg! *Wisps of hearth smoke waft from the village rooftops.* Run! Get away! *But her warnings are like whispers on the breeze, answered only by barbs of sinister laughter stabbing inside her head . . .*

Sap

*L*ia awoke from her fate-dream with tangled hair and a kinked neck. Another foretelling, and this time the monstrous *Straif* lurked on the fringes of Rockberg. They had to hurry, had to get back before—

"Ruddy fiend!" Wynn's voice jerked Lia upright.

Her eyes rounded as Wynn plunged his sword deep into a squirming blob of mud. Loud gurgling uttered from the badger-sized glob, the oozing anomaly flailing a pair of spindly arms before it finally went still.

"Ba . . . Ballybog," Lia shrieked, scrambling from the ground.

Another ballybog lurched forth, attaching itself to Nolan's back leg. Like a pulsing clot, the bog goblin clung on and emitted hideous slurping noises. Nolan squealed and reared, and tried to scale the mountainside.

"Grab his reins," Wynn shouted.

Lia leapt forward and grasped the ropes. She tried to pull Nolan from his frenzied climbing, but the horse was too panicked. Her shoulders burned from her efforts and she struggled to maintain her footing. Wynn jabbed his blade through the ballybog's side. Its arms flayed and green slime drizzled from its body before it dropped from Nolan's leg.

A third ballybog rose from the marsh and careened against the hillside, landing at Lia's feet. She kicked furiously at it, but the creature reared up, revealing red eyes and gnashing teeth. It lunged at her, as if on springs, and she ducked just in time. She clawed at the mountainside to get away, but a cold weight landed on her back and pointed teeth pierced into her skin. Her mouth opened in a silent gasp.

She fell backward as Wynn skewered the monster. He flung the creature back into the mire and reached for Lia.

"We've gotta move!" Wynn scooped her up like a rag doll and lifted her onto Merrie. He gave the mare a slap on the rump, and Lia gripped the reins with waning strength.

Merrie had somehow escaped attack, though her neck trembled and shone with sweat as she trampled across the wetland. Fear drove both horses to dash across the marsh, their pace swift until the outlying moor gave way to blankets of grass and heather. Though her eyes blurred with pain, Lia spotted the open crown of a *Saille* tree beneath the dawning sky.

"The . . . willow," she muttered.

They neared the tree and came upon a brook. A measure of relief filled Lia at the sight of clean water. She slid from Merrie's back, knelt down, and drew up her cloak and tunic, exposing her back.

Wynn sucked in his breath. "Ooh, Lee—"

"It's too wet for a fire . . . and we need to . . . treat the wounds properly." She hissed in pain while Wynn scrubbed at the bloody ooze. When he finished, she took a deep breath and stumbled away.

"Where are you going?" Wynn yelled.

"Just wait . . . need it to heal." Lia discarded her cloak, remaining clad only in her pale green tunic, tanned breeches, and leather boots. She cinched her belt tighter around her waist and, gritting her teeth, reached up and twisted her hair into a closely fastened bun.

She crept toward the *Saille* tree, hearing the familiar buzz of worker bees flying through the leaves. She knew their hive was full of honeycomb, ready for the impending winter. As long as she took only a small portion of their food, it would not jeopardize them. But they would still guard their stores.

No fire meant no smoker to calm the bees. Without the distraction of smoke, Lia would have to depend solely on her skills. Before getting closer to the hive, she wielded her knife and cut down a long stem. The wood tingled against her skin, filling her with its essence. Less grand than the *Nion*, but no less profound, the lissome *Saille* emanated within her mind a cascade of healing rain, its cool waters washing away some of her distress. The worst of her pain ebbed, and she gazed in awe at the tree.

"Many thanks," she whispered. She folded one of its leaves into her mouth, and then wound the flexuous withy lasso-like under her belt.

The honeybees seemed unconcerned by her presence, so far. Lia inched toward the outer lining of the hive. A few bees eyed her, their tiny heads following her movements. Guard bees, she knew. They would alert the others of danger.

"Greetings, sweet sisters," she said, chewing on the bitter leaf.

Koun came to mind, her hound beside her whenever she tended her bee skeps back home. Oddly, the numerous honeybees buzzing in and out of the double-decker hives never bothered him. Lia always thought her strange dog was part bee. She wished he was here with her now.

She reached up and cut a piece of honeycomb from the edge of the hive. Numerous bees buzzed around the stolen treasure. Several hit her chest in warning. She backed away and placed the chunk of comb into an empty pouch tied to her belt. With the honey unexposed, and with her timely retreat, she escaped from being followed or stung.

Bee-charmer, that's what Granda called her, someone who had the skill to enter a hive without provoking attack. It had taken years of practice and an undying interest in the traits of bees. Even then, she'd had her fair share of stings. Such was the life of a bee-charmer.

Lia was shivering by the time she made it back to Wynn. "Let's . . . move ahead. I don't want to expose their honey . . . so close to the hive."

"Put this on. What were you thinking?" Wynn wrapped her cloak around her shoulders.

Her shivers calmed. "Had to leave it. Cloak's too dark and furry, like a predator."

Wynn helped her up onto Merrie and she grabbed the reins to keep from swooning. Though Wynn had scrubbed her puncture wounds clean, they ran deep and began oozing again. Nolan didn't fare any better. Lia spotted the wounds on his fleshy hindquarter, and even with the blood and slime washed away, they continued to seep down his leg. She knew if his wounds festered, he'd be doomed.

The moor sprawled before them toward the wooded horizon. The mountain relaxed into rolling hills, dotted with hawthorn and oak trees. Sporadic rays of mid-morning sun shone through the haze, helping to allay the chill seeping into Lia's bones.

Wynn led them up a hill to a fruit-filled hawthorn, or *Huath* tree, and dismounted Nolan. "Ground's dry enough here, I think. I can make a small fire for you to brew herbs."

Lia folded another pain-relieving *Saille* leaf into her mouth and chewed it with vigor. "No need for a fire. We can use the honey on the wounds for now."

She clenched her teeth, desperately hoping the bog goblins hadn't plagued them with some incurable poison. She should have known in this enchanted land to watch for trickster creatures roaming the bog. The old tales were full of ballybogs, marsh naiads, and will-o'the-wisps, clever fiends wreaking havoc on their quarry. With any luck, there'd be no further travel through perilous fens.

She eased off Merrie and opened her pouch. She broke off a piece of the honeycomb and handed it to Wynn, eyeing the punctures in his hand. "Squeeze some on your wounds, then do the same on my back. Be sure to smear it on real thick."

Wynn did as she asked, securing his handiwork with strips of nettle cloth before doing the same on Nolan's leg. The horse snorted, but held still while Wynn tied the cloth around his trembling thigh. Afterward, Nolan licked the remaining sweetness from his master's hand.

"We can rest a bit. The sun's barely up—" Wynn started to say.

"We have to keep moving." Lia swallowed her second helping of honeycomb, a measure of strength seeping back into her body. "I had another fate-dream last night, Wynn."

Wynn peered at her. "What about?"

"I dreamed the *Straif* neared the edge of Rockberg. It's no longer keeping to the Bryns."

"You're sure it wasn't just—never mind. I trust your visions."

Lia warmed at his faith in her. "There's something else, too. Since the *Nion* tree, I've been feeling, well, I can sense the trees. It just happened with that willow—the *Saille* tree. And back at the *Fearns* my mind reached all the way through one, far down into its roots, and even out into the stream."

Wynn's brow rose and Lia added, "That's when I heard Grandma Mryna. She told me to find her at the headless *Eadha* where the black waters roil."

His eyes rounded. "Grandma?"

"They took her life, Wynn. I saw her image in the river on our way to the *Nion*, and then she came again in that stream last night. Somehow she's reaching out through Brume's waters."

"How could her soul . . . ? I thought . . ." Wynn shook his head and let out a long sigh. "I don't know what to think anymore, Lee. Everyday our journey becomes more twisted. We've gotten ourselves deep in this shadow-land."

Lia knew they had to go deeper, still.

Wynn started to turn away, but then rummaged in his cloak and pulled out a worn scroll. "You dropped this at the stream, must've fallen from your tunic when I was washing your wounds."

"Oh, I found it hidden inside Granda's cane after he fell. It's a page torn from Grandma's book. I know it by heart now, but you go ahead and read it. Maybe you can make some sense of it."

Wynn unfolded the parchment and read out the script,

A child of imposing grace will shine for all the land;
From moon to moon she will race, as armies take their stand.
Across the kingdom her foe will chase,
As her soul strives to stay free,
And in the end her freedom resides
Within the great hallowed tree.

"Armies? Hallowed tree?" Wynn blew out his breath, rolled the page back up, and handed it to her. "Another impossible riddle."

Yeah, she thought, *I'm beginning to grow weary of them myself.*

Before Lia mounted Merrie, she eyed the *Huath* tree. Ma used the tart red haws to make jams. Lia and Granda gathered the flowering tops and berries for blends to help the aged. Curious, Lia reached up and touched the shiny green leaves, and immediately felt the rush.

A warm sensation ran through her body, as if a springtime sun caressed her insides. Her thoughts whirled with ribbons and lace, the scent of flowers, and velvety grass beneath her feet. Kelven appeared in her mind with his soft hazel eyes and easy smile. He beckoned to her, reaching out his arms until he folded them around her. He nuzzled her hair and ran his hand through its length. Then he tilted her head back and his lips came down upon hers, warm, gentle, sending ripples of pleasure though her body. . . .

"Lee?" Wynn asked.

Lia let go of the leaves and stepped away from the *Huath* tree.

Wynn cocked his head. "You look all flushed."

"I . . . it's nothing." She averted her eyes and mounted Merrie, and then trotted her down the hill.

The crisp air cooled Lia's burning face. She racked her mind until she finally remembered the verse in Grandma's book under the sketch of a hawthorn tree:

> *Lovely* Huath *with flowers of cream,*
> *Place of enchanted wedding dreams;*
> *Lovely whitethorn where maidens blush bright*

Under springtime love and all its delight.

Well, no wonder, she thought. She'd be sure to recall the lore of the next tree before she connected with it. Such a profound mark the *Great Nion* had left. Its brief embrace bestowed a mighty gift. Even without touching them, Lia sensed a subtle animation from the trees dotting the hillside.

If Granda Luis could see me now. A spring of tears tumbled down her cheeks. *Hold strong Granda, just a little longer.*

They made haste across the valley to the woodland, which served as a home to many. A herd of roe deer charged across the hills into the dense forest, a pair of red fox eyed them before slinking away, and birds warbled and chirped amid the trees.

They traversed the bracken and scrub growing beneath oak and beech trees. The multitude of trees emanated an array of energies, and Lia had to subdue the sensations rushing through her all at once. She breathed deeply and focused her mind's eye on the trees closest to her.

The kingly oaks and queenly beeches seemed to carry on a marriage. The exposed beech roots dipped down at the base of the oaks, their woody arms entwined in a loving embrace. The trees exuded harmony, like a family working together. As in the *Fearn* grove, countless tree fae watched them. Their golden bodies dipped in and out like rivulets of sap through the autumnal trees, and though Lia reveled in the unity of the forest, she couldn't ignore the mounting pain on her back.

She knew the bitter *Saille* leaves and honey fought a poison beyond their healing powers. She'd need to stop soon and get that fire going after all. *A dry patch in the woods*, she figured, *where we can rest while I brew a stronger remedy.*

Her mouth grew dry, and she drained her water skin only to find herself thirsty for more. The forest began to blur and sway, as if submerged under water. Lia closed her eyes in the hopes of clearing her vision, but opened them to find the green of the forest turned silver.

What's happening to me?

She licked her lips, dry as summer soil, and opened her mind to the grove. The trees grasped her thoughts and filled her head with a single word: River.

Lia clenched her teeth against the pain and nudged Merrie forward to Nolan's flank. "Wynn, we need to get to the riv—"

"Lee!" Wynn cried out as Lia fell forward.

He grabbed around her torso and pulled her off Merrie. His voice came in clips. "I'll get—somewhere—fire—need to wash—" Then darkness swallowed all sound.

She swam in an ocean of pitch, her body burning in agony. Nothing but hollow cries escaped her mouth. She fought against the darkness, struggling to escape its grasp, and then the sound of rushing waters whispered promises of comfort.

She felt the cold, solid ground beneath her, though her head rested on something soft. Her eyes fluttered open to the gray sky. "I

123

hear water."

"You're awake!" Wynn's face came into view. "Thank the fallow fields. You've been moaning and carrying on, and you're burning up with fever. I've gotten us to dry ground, and I'm going to start a fire and get your kettle going."

The sound of rapids grew louder upon Lia's ears, summoning her to them. "The river," she whispered.

"Yes, we're on a riverbank, but the water's, well, something's wrong with it, Lee. It shines, like quicksilver." Wynn drew up his hand and pushed back his blond shag. The wounds on his hand had turned black and oozed with pus.

"Your hand." Lia reached out to him, forcing her head and shoulders off the ground. She fell back, nearly fainting again from the pain that roared down her back.

"Lee, stay still. Let me get the kettle going, and then you can tell me what herbs to put in. Don't move. I'll be right back with some firewood." Wynn hurried into the woods.

Lia turned her gaze toward the river. She gritted her teeth and slowly rolled her body over on all fours. Her flesh burned in agony, as if someone had poured boiling tar on it, and darkness threatened her mind once more. She willed herself to stay conscious and crawled on hands and knees to the river. The silver waters filled her with hope, and her body and soul yearned to partake of them. Her breath quickened. She dipped her hand into the cool liquid. Then she touched her fingers to her lips and tasted the droplets.

"Lee, no! It could be poisonous, enchanted." Wynn dropped the bundle of wood and darted to her side.

She sat upright, her pain vanished, and she smiled. "Oh, it's enchanted. See for yourself. I've never felt so good."

Lia nodded eagerly and he bent down and tasted for himself. His face beamed. "I feel like I could run for days."

Lia drank more from her cupped hands, allowing the water's metallic taste to linger in her mouth before she swallowed it. Her senses heightened to the colors and smells of the forest surrounding her, and every muscle in her body sung with vitality. She grabbed the empty water skin hanging from her wrap belt and filled it with the silver waters. Then she retrieved her spares.

Wynn followed her lead. "Maybe keep a few with regular water," he remarked, refilling half his skins and leaving the others intact.

Nolan limped to the shining river, sniffed it, and then drank his fill. Merrie followed suit. Like young foals, they started to prance about, Nolan giving no care to his bandaged leg. Lia and Wynn smiled at their horses' sudden frolicking.

"Wynn, your hand." His rotting wounds had disappeared.

"Check mine." Lia threw off her cloak and turned her back toward Wynn. He carefully removed the protective cloth and wiped the honey away.

"They're gone. Every wound, like they were never there."

"It was after I drank," she said. "All the pain disappeared."

"What *is* this river? Where does it come from?" Wynn wondered aloud.

"I don't know. I don't recall anything written about it. Hey, let's check Nolan."

The horse's wounds had healed as well.

"We could take this water home, Lee," Wynn said with eyes bright. "Use it to heal your da and Granda, and all the others."

Lia bit her lip. "I'm sure the water would do wonders for the people, but if it's really all that's needed to cure the *Straif's* poison, then why didn't Ebrill, or the tree wyrm, or any of the *Nion* guardians say so? I'm afraid we're dealing with something stronger than a bog goblin's bane."

Wynn pursed his lips, as if mulling over Lia's words. "Guess you're right. I'd hate to take a chance on it not working."

With a shrug, he glanced back at the river. "The water's too rough here. I say we get upstream, find a place to cross."

They rallied the horses and sped up the riverbank while the sun ran its course behind a gray sky. For hours, they trudged up the steepening terrain, but the river roared impassable beside them.

Wynn drew Nolan closer to Lia. "We're edging the mountains again. The river has to narrow soon—"

"Look there!" Lia nudged Merrie into a gallop toward an immense oak, or *Duir* tree. It grew alone on the crest of a knoll and displayed a cluster of golden bough amid its crown.

Wynn hurried after her and waited at the edge of the *Duir's* canopy while Lia placed her hand on its rough bark. Oak lore ran heavily through the *Grimoire*, the tree honored for its protection and strength. Thoughts of Da and Granda, of Uncle Finn, and even Doc Lloyd filled her mind. Like fathers of the woodlands, oak trees endured the trials of time.

"See that cluster up there, Wynn? It's another ingredient for the elixir," Lia said. "Fetch me a long rope, my bow, and a bolt."

Wynn did as she asked without question. Lia tied the rope to one of her crossbow bolts, placed it in the groove on the stock, and shot it into the middle of the golden bough. With a quick yank, the clinging fungus tumbled down, its olive green leaves and white berries a welcome sight. Lia scooped up her prize and handed it to Wynn.

"Pack some up while I give thanks," she said, and placed her hands back on the trunk. She imparted her gratitude, and then as she started to pull away, a strange energy pricked at her mind.She used her thoughts to penetrate deeper, reaching down through the sturdy trunk, down into the roots. An aroma of rich musk filled her senses. Like a heart, the tree's energy beat in rhythm. But another beat resounded, its drum smaller, low, and deep.

A flash of light and a loud crack tore through Lia's mind, and before she could blink, Wynn tackled her to the ground.

He coughed as he lifted himself off her. Lia sputtered, "Wha . . . what happened?"

"Lightning. It struck the top branch. I thought you'd be burned for sure." Wynn struggled to catch his breath while several rain droplets fell on his face.

Lia stood up and noticed a thin stream of smoke rising from the top of the *Duir*. Otherwise, the tree appeared unharmed.

"Before the lightning hit," she said, "I heard something inside the tree that wasn't a part of it—"

A loud rustling came from behind the *Duir*. Wynn gripped his sword and took a fighting stance. An ancient face poked out from around the tree. Lia's heart skipped. The creature displayed a long white beard and eyes of aquamarine. He gaped at them, and then stepped from behind the tree to reveal his short, stocky build and iron axe.

Lia found her voice and uttered, "Dwarf."

Hedge

ven with that grand hollow, sure is hard to get a nap in with that blasted lightning. Good thing this old *Duir's* got tough skin," the dwarf grunted, patting the tree. "Name's Gobann. Heard you were wandering these parts. Thought I'd stick around and get a look-see."

"You're a dwarf." Lia knew she stated the obvious and had never doubted the legends, but she still marveled at meeting one from the ancient race.

"Aye, last time I checked, but you never know what can happen in a place like this. About eighty years ago, my scouting partner got himself turned into coal. Tangled up with some crazy imp he did, but that's a whole other story. A'course we fired him into a real nice diamond, but 'tis not quite the same now is it?"

Wynn shot a glance at Lia. He held his sword awkwardly and shifted his feet back and forth, as if unsure whether Gobann was a friend or foe.

"Gobann," Lia said, "are there many others?"

"A'course. Got a whole passel o'clans deep in the mountains. 'Tis only a few of us scouts ever come into the valley though, to keep on eye on things." Gobann leaned on his axe and stroked his snowy beard. His eyes sparkled like polished gems, revealing wisdom far deeper than his polite bantering let on.

"If you're trying to cross the Seren River, you'll have to go through the *Coll* grove. Only about a half day's journey up these hills, if you're interested o'course." A smile tugged at his lips.

"You know where we're headed. Then you must know about the *Straif.*" Hope filled Lia. "Do you know how we might defeat it? Oh, we've just come from the *Nion* tree and the woman said something about using Brume's blood, but I don't understand what she meant, and there's parts to the elixir I've been trying to figure out—"

"Mine ears, you're all in a whirl. 'Fraid I'm just a scout, don't know much about 'lixers or spells, unless you'd be wanting a stone charmed. That's what dwarfs do best, you know."

"Of course! The dwarfs had cared for Rockberg's quartz towers." Lia pulled at the leather thong and brought out her pouch. She quickly opened it and dumped the stone onto her palm. "You can help me with this."

"By thunder's hammer!" Gobann fell to his knees. "A piece, cast from an ancient one. How's it so?"

Lia shook her head. "I don't know how it broke free. I thought maybe because the stones had gotten so old."

"May I hold it?" Gobann lifted his eyes to hers.

"Lee, wait." Wynn stepped in front of her. "What kinda rock is this anyway?"

"Please, brave warrior, my people spent thousands o'years caring for these rocks, as you kindly put it. On my honor I'll not harm it, nor steal it away."

"It's all right, Wynn," Lia said, maneuvering around him. "It's just like in the legends. I believe he speaks true."

She handed the quartz to the kneeling dwarf. He held it as if it were a fragile egg, caressing it ever so softly. All at once, the stone lit up. Lia's jaw dropped. The light radiated outward, enveloping the dwarf's hand. Heat pulsated from it, and the white glow turned to beams of colors.

Lia's awe was intensified by the *Duir* tree's response. Its essence drummed within her like a strong pulse. She was sure the tree leaned closer to the crystal's light.

The dwarf placed the stone back onto Lia's palm and its light subsided. "That's as much as I can do, 'tis your stone after all. Crystals use receptive magic, you know. Like mirrors, reflecting out what you put in. I could tell this one dwelt in an herber garden, humming with all sorts o'fae."

"Fae? But, it came from my home, back in Rockberg." Lia

dropped her stone back in its pouch.

"The fae are the few that remain hidden in your world, though they only stick around in the best o'gardens." The dwarf winked at her and stroked his beard. "That quartz'll wield a lot more magic with the right skill, if you're interested o'course. Could also help us dwarfs answer a few questions."

"What are you proposing?" Wynn asked with a tight jaw.

Gobann's face wrinkled into a smile. "I'm sure our smiths'd forge you the finest o'blades if you decide to come back with me."

Wynn's eyes grew wide. "Back with you? We're racing against time as it is, a trek through those mountains would take—"

"'Bout as long as it takes to fry up some trout, and that'd be sounding real good now. Mica, my wife, soaks them in a milk bath first and then—"

"Magic!" Lia's pulse raced.

"Her cooking? Mica'd be pleased to hear that." Gobann grinned playfully before he turned serious. "Aye, lass, 'tis magic that'll get us there, or something like it. Have to leave your beasts here though; they won't likely fit. But not to worry, we'll be back in a wink, and they'll have company."

Fit? Lia wondered if she'd heard him right.

The dwarf whistled through two thick fingers, and within minutes, a pure white mare charged up the hill. Merrie and Nolan scampered like two foals to greet her. Lia figured their drinks at the river still had them extra lively. The mare nosed their horses before halting at the dwarf's side.

"This here's Gypsum. She's a right friend, and she'll keep a good watch on both o'yours. Saved her several years back when she was stuck in the mire. Would have died if I hadn't pulled her from that sludge. Now, she's always 'round when I need her." Gobann turned and whispered into Gypsum's ear, her lobe twitching. Nolan nudged against the mare's flank with nostrils aflare.

Lia stared at Gypsum. The horse's beauty stirred something deep within her. She exuded grace and purity, as if she was as unsullied as her pristine white coat.

"Follow me." The dwarf waved for them to follow as he turned back toward the tree.

Wynn stood his ground and Lia nudged him. "Wynn, we have to go with him. The legends tell of their stone mage skills. They can show me how to wield the quartz—"

"I don't care what the legends say, Lee." He gripped her shoulders, his eyes shining with unease. "Think about it. Who drove them from their homes all those years ago? It was our kind, and now here we are, coming into their homeland again. I say we take our leave, get across the river to the eastern wood, and finish this journey on our own."

"What if we can't do this on our own?" Heat rose into Lia's neck. "What if their magic could give us a way to defend ourselves, maybe even put an end to the *Straif*?"

Her words put an extra furrow in Wynn's brow, and before he

could argue she added, "You said it yourself: farming and sword fighting haven't done you much good here. To have any chance at all, we need to gain other skills, other weapons. Weapons of magic."

Wynn blew out his breath and shook his head. "Fine. We'll do it your way."

He moved aside, sheathed his blade, and followed Lia to where Gobann stood before a hollow on the back of the *Duir* tree.

Gobann appeared to stretch taller and pride sparkled from his eyes. "Only two o'these passages in all the land and this'n' belongs to the dwarfs."

Lia peered into the hollow, and understanding struck her like a bolt of lightning. "A portal."

"You could call it that. But *Duir's Run* is what we call it."

"Wait a minute," Wynn said. "We're going inside the tree?"

"Aye, lad, 'tis a fine passage. You'll see."

"You mentioned two. Where's the other *Duir's Run?*" Lia asked.

"Ah, you'll not be wanting to venture into the likes o'that one. 'Tis no *Duir* neither, but an ancient *Idho*, timekeeper, bridge to the Otherworld. Get lost in a tree like that. Never knew no one who went in to come back out." Gobann stepped into the hollow. "No tricks with the *Duir* here; 'tis loyal and true. Might have to duck a bit though, you both being so tall."

Hmm. The other portal is a yew tree. How strange that her special tree, the place she nestled in for hours back in the Bryns, was also an *Idho*. She and Koun spent many hours snoozing in the cozy hollow, ever since she first found her pup sleeping there.

She took a deep breath and turned to Wynn. "Ready?"

Despite his wariness, he replied, "Lead the way."

Lia followed the dwarf's steps into the *Duir*, ducking her head slightly and adjusting her knapsack. Wynn nearly doubled over to fit under the ceiling and his muffled swears echoed through the passage.

In the dim light, Lia drew in the pungent scent of the tree, a mix of earth and fire. She followed Gobann into a tunnel, dragging her hand across the coarse walls. The *Duir* answered her touch with a sensation of power. It was not the kind of power to lord over others, but rather a strength igniting her resolve. She relaxed in its peace, confident that answers lie ahead.

"Spades, it's shrinking," Wynn yelped in the narrowing tunnel.

"Almost there, young warrior," Gobann called back, leading them deeper into the passage.

The tree's inner ridges gave way to a cold, rock-like surface against Lia's hands. A rhythmic knocking echoed from a distance. "What's that noise?"

"That'd be the miners' hammers 'n'picks. Our caves are full of minerals: agate, carnelian, fluorite, and a dark green beryl you'd know as emerald, just to name a few."

The hammering grew louder as the tunnel walls opened into a stone grotto. Torches glimmered around the cave, revealing a rounded chamber with a wooden table and chairs in the center. Lia's palm grew wet against rivulets of water running down the smooth stone. The air grew chilly and she pulled her cloak tighter.

Wynn unfolded himself from the tunnel and stood upright in the room, glowering.

"I'll be needing to announce you. Stay put for a bit." Gobann disappeared through a stout wooden door on the far wall.

"Well, I hope you're right," Wynn said. "We're nothing but fish in a barrel now."

"Gobann wants to help us," Lia countered.

Wynn paced the floor, shaking his head. "The more I think about it, the more I believe the dwarfs know all about that *Straif* tree and are glad it's attacking us. It's the perfect revenge. Maybe they sent Gobann as a diversion, to stop us from defeating it."

His worries jabbed at Lia's resolve. Certainly, Wynn had reason to be anxious. They'd encountered their share of obstacles in Brume already, and time was ticking away. But the *Grimoire* didn't speak ill of dwarfs. The only passages told of ancient times when they lived in the lands before humans. And honesty had shone from Gobann's eyes. She was sure of it.

"We're hardly some army here to root them out," Lia said, trying to sound confident. "Besides, we're different, the fae know our kin, and Grandma was special. Gobann might have even known her."

Wynn frowned, but then his eyes lifted and Lia knew they were no longer alone.

She whirled around to find four bearded dwarfs staring back at her. Gobann stood next to another his size, who stood next to two shorter dwarfs each holding steaming platters.

"I never had the pleasure o'meeting your kinswoman, but Haegl, another scout, did. He's retired now o'course, but that's a whole other story. Anyhow, sit and have some freshers." Gobann motioned toward the table.

The two shorter dwarfs carried the platters to the table, and then ushered Lia and Wynn to sit in front of the feast. Lia's unease subsided amid their kindliness, and her mouth watered at the smell of smoked salmon and roasted pheasant garnished with onions, leeks, and turnips. There were glazed apples and honeyed walnuts, freshly baked bread slathered in butter, and rounds of white cheese, all accompanied by goblets of wine. And in the center of it all was a bowl of tiny . . . *rubies?*

"Just a small snack before the evening meal. The rubies are a might tart, try 'em with the apples." Gobann winked. "Like you to meet the greeting crew. This here's Schorl, respected clan sage, and these two fine ladies are in charge of guests."

Ladies with beards?

"Oh, well, I'm Lia and this is my cousin, Wynn." Lia was relieved by their hospitality, yet baffled by their appearance and taste for precious stones. She slipped off her knapsack and reached for some pheasant. When she looked up, her eyes caught numerous small gemstones glittering from the two female dwarfs' beards. Wynn gaped at the women's facial hair, which rivaled his da's.

"Thank you, ladies, Gobann. I should like to have a word in

private now." Schorl waved his bejeweled hand in command. His beard hung in salt and pepper braids against smooth pale skin.

He's younger than Gobann and definitely less outdoorsy, but he's their royal sage.

"I'll just be a quick shout away if you need me." Gobann followed the lady dwarfs through the door.

Schorl remained, peering down on them, and Lia supposed he stiffened his spine to appear taller. It seemed as if hooks tugged at the corners of his lips, pulling them into a smile. His words came slow and deliberate, "Been a while since our scouts reported humans in the land. Not since your elder was spotted about ten years ago."

"Our granda stopped coming here," Lia said. "Nemetona's Royal Guard began patrolling the edge of fog, and a few years after that, Granda's legs went bad. He only returned, and brought us here with him, out of desperate need."

She took a quick sip of wine and continued, "Maybe you already know, but a *Straif* tree's breached the fog, attacking and poisoning our people. It attacked Granda here in Brume, in the forest edging the fae meadow. We're gathering ingredients for the cure, and somehow we have to get a piece from the *Straif*—"

"And the stone?" he interrupted.

"Uh, yes, the quartz. I've been trying to figure out how it works. It grows warm when I touch it, and I've dreamed of it burning bright, but I've not been able to light it up on my own." She drew the stone out of her pouch and displayed it on her opened palm.

Schorl's eyes glinted and his tongue flickered across his lips, as if he was about to strike. Before either of them moved, Wynn scooped up the crystal. "So, are you the one going to teach her how to wield magic from it?"

A flash of anger crossed Schorl's face and he sneered. "I'm not going do anything except leave you to your meal. Just needed to see it myself, make sure Gobann had it right. What happens next is up to the clan chief." Schorl turned on his heel and left the cave.

"See what I mean?" Wynn shot an icy glance at Lia and handed her back the quartz. "That clan sage is trouble."

Lia gnawed on some bread. She wished Gobann would return. She didn't like that he was sent away. He seemed to know enough about stones, at least enough to show her a few tricks. She'd ask him as soon as he returned, and then they could hurry back to the foothills through the *Duir*.

The door burst open and Lia watched for Gobann to enter, but was soon disappointed at the sight of four armored dwarfs. Wynn grabbed his blade and kicked his chair against the wall behind him, his eyes darting to each of the guards.

"No need to panic, boy; just a formality," one dwarf grumbled.

Lia hovered at the tunnel entrance. "Where's Gobann?"

Wynn teetered on his feet and his head lolled forward. Lia leapt toward him, but her head went dizzy, and her vision turned to mud.

Kindling

There now. 'Twas only a bit of m'woozy brew, just enough t'get you t'our inner city without knowing how you got here. You're of the human race, after all." The female voice sounded far away, as if it echoed through a tunnel.

Lia's eyes focused on the tiny room and she found her throat dry when she spoke. "The poison you used . . . the bells or the shade?"

"Ah, you know the dark ones. Give you a hint: Her leaves do reek, and her fruit'll bite, and she dangles trumpets of vespertine white."

Lia was in no mood for riddles. She knew the answer, but her head ached and she didn't want to play solve-the-riddle. The dwarf moved closer, yellow gems sparkling from her beard.

"You were part of our greeting crew, right? In charge of *guests*? Where's Wynn, my cousin?"

"In good hands, not t'worry. Like I said, 'twas a simple act of caution." She handed Lia a mug of water. "Drink this; it'll help."

Lia studied the water. It appeared clear and scentless, and her mouth yearned for it. She drank it down, the cool liquid washing the bitter taste from her mouth.

"Your guides are waiting for you." The dwarf ambled to the door and opened it. Grunts and throat clearing echoed from the hall.

Lia got up from the bed and steadied her footing, and caught sight of her knapsack draped on a stool. The flap of her pack was undone, and she glared at the nosy dwarf before slinging it over her back.

"I'll see you at suppertime," her hostess said, as if drugging guests was nothing to blink twice about.

I'd like to try a few woozy brews on her and see how she likes it.

"Mouse holes," Lia clipped, stooping through the curved doorway where two armored dwarfs met her. Thick beards covered half their faces and they both wore steel chest plates etched with a wingless, two-legged dragon.

Wingless? Like the tree wyrm, more snake than dragon.

"Follow me," one ordered while the other took his stance behind her. The three strode in silence through the tunnel. Wall torches cast shadows against the stone, and aside from their footsteps, the passageway was quiet. Nerve-fraying quiet.

After endless twists and turns, they rounded a corner and came upon a door bigger than the usual mouse holes. With a nudge from the dwarf behind her, Lia opened the door to a blaze of sunlight. She stepped forward with her eyes shaded to help them adjust, and a shiver crossed her shoulders from the crisp mountain air. Her vision focused and she gasped. A stone courtyard sprawled into a maze of paths winding around towers of quartz. *Towers of quartz!*

"That'll do, that'll do, run along, she's in my care now." A dwarf with wild white hair and a beard to match scuttled toward them. Thick eyeglasses hung crooked on his nose and his eyebrows looked as if they might take flight.

The guards turned back toward the tunnel, but stopped at the sound of commotion coming from inside. The door burst open, its wood nearly splintering, and Wynn tumbled into the courtyard.

"Get your grubby hands off me!" Anger flushed his face. He steadied himself and charged back at the guards.

"Wynn," Lia yelped.

Though he doubled their height, he might as well have been tackling a brick wall. The dwarfs pushed him away with such force he crashed into a table of rusted shields.

"Wrestle with that awhile, youngling." One of the guards tossed Wynn's sheathed sword onto the ground beside him. "He's all yours," the guard grumbled before following the others into the tunnel.

Lia reached down to him. "Are you all right?"

He lifted himself out of the mess of shields. The clang of metal hitting metal rang through courtyard. "Half-witted, stinking, hairy stumps—the lot of them! I knew this was a bad idea, knew that stub, Schorl, was trouble—" Wynn stopped short.

The elder dwarf stared at him, wide-eyed and trembling.

"Oh, he didn't mean you," Lia jumped in. "Just those pushy guards and that clan sage. We were poisoned, well not really *poisoned*, but definitely robbed of our wits."

Wynn's voice softened and he stepped closer to the old dwarf. "I meant no harm to you, but Lee's right—we're being treated like prisoners here."

The snow-headed dwarf relaxed and a smile grew on his face. "Ah well, Schorl's never been one for tact. But prisoners you're not, else you'd be hung by your toes by now. No, you're special. You carry something very special, and you can be sure the whole clan— even the whole race—is talking about it by now."

Wynn shrugged and bent down to retrieve his sword. He began picking up the strewn shields.

"Oh, leave them. Just keep the one and follow me. This is quite amazing really; wondered if I'd live long enough t'learn the fate of our ancient stones, and here you are, the key t'all our questions right in your hands." The dwarf waved for them to follow. "Name's Laguz by the way, head crystallographer in charge of these here quartz."

Lia gazed at the glassy facets sparkling in the sunlight, her head awash in memories of Rockberg. These towers appeared fresher, or maybe just cleaner, than the ones back home. She and Wynn followed Laguz to one of the great stones with a large table set next to it. Upon the table were a variety of swords and armor, gemstones of all colors, and glass bottles filled with mysterious liquids.

"Come, come. Oh, the excitement! Now, dear, would you be so kind as t'show it t'me?"

Lia eyed Wynn, his face painted with concern, and she withdrew her crystal. Its familiar warmth spread over her palm and she peeled her fingers away to expose it.

"Keep hold of it, 'tis your stone after all. I'll just rest my hand on top. Might help if you close your eyes t'start."

Lia hesitated, then closed her eyes and felt the dwarf's hand come down. The sensation was immediate. The stone burned, barely tolerable against her flesh, its light blazing through the walls of her eyelids. *Ohhh.*

"Do you feel it?"

"I feel it burning—"

"Not on your hand; you got t'feel it in your mind, in your heart."

Lia paused in concentration. She had become used to feeling the trees, sensing their energy. *How can the quartz be much different?* She reached out with her mind and immediately understood the difference. Trees varied in age, some as old as ancient times, but rocks were timeless. From the celestial birth of the planet grew minerals, and from earth's fiery blood, igneous rocks formed. The precious creations existed long before life roamed the lands and were sure to remain long after life perished. Lia surged with excitement. It was as if she held a piece of the starry sky right in the palm of her hand.

"Good. Excellent. Truly amazing for a non-dwarf. Never knew 'twas possible. Now, child, deep within your mind, kindly ask the crystal t'show you a bit of its recent memory."

"Uh, all right." She felt awkward, but focused her thoughts on the request, and a fuzzy image began forming in her mind.

"You've got it," Laguz said, pressing his hand on the stone. "Now, let it become clearer."

She drew in her breath and held the image, and all at once, a flood of pictures spilled forth. From present time, the pictures ran backward, speedy clips of village life flashing before her. She watched the people come and go like heedless cattle, blind to anything but their daily routines, ignorant to the workings of magic towering on their hillsides. They viewed the great towers as nothing more than an annoying, yet immovable, part of the landscape.

A pang of regret for her people's disregard shot through Lia. For so long the crystals stood among humans, hovering at the fringes of their lives, barely noticed by them, and never honored. For a while, the luculent stones drew vitality from the plants and insects, and an occasional passerby who bestowed them a glance. However, with time's incessant chisel, the enchanted quartz fell mute, asleep with the same apathy they'd been doled out. That is, until Lia's garden danced spirals of herbs and fae around one of them, and the sparkling centerpiece awoke with renewed fervor.

Her stone whizzed her further backward in time and a flood of happiness poured into her. The pictures slowed as the crystal lingered on its memories. The land appeared untouched, innocent. All of the towers beamed auras of light and a flurry of activity wrapped the base of each one. Numerous dwarfs tended their glassy gods. With silken cloths, some polished the vitreous faces while others placed thick hands on them, sending dwarf magic deep into the stones. Weapons, gems, water skins, and bowls of herbs and vegetables bathed in the crystalline glow.

"The items? Why do they put them all there?" Lia whispered.

"Hold on t'your connection, child. Open your eyes slowly, and I'll show you."

Lia drew her eyelids up and found herself encapsulated in light. Her breath slid from her mouth.

"Wynn, is it? All right, lad, I want you t'hand your sword over t'your cousin."

"Uh, okay." Wynn entered the bright sphere and set the hilt of his sword into Lia's free hand. Then he stepped back.

The heat from the quartz shot through Lia's body, up through her arm, into her torso, and down to her palm holding Wynn's sword. She vibrated with energy, riding wave after wave of radiant power. After a few moments, the tide subsided and the stone's light dimmed. She held the sword out to her cousin.

Wynn's eyes rounded at his glowing blade. He wrapped his hands around the hilt and the blade's light intensified. "Whoa! It's like a beam of sunlight."

"Ah," Laguz smiled, "I see you've both got the touch. Lia's ignited the blade, and now you, as the sword's master, have brightened its flame. This one'll cut through anything now, and I do mean anything. Keep it sheathed 'til you really need it. Always show your blade respect, and it'll return the favor tenfold. Metal's like that, you know."

His eyes sparkled at Lia. "Now, lass, let's see what you can do with that ol' shield."

Lia repeated the process, holding the shield in her other hand while the heat moved through her. This transformation took less time. The rusty, dented shield fired to perfect steel, emblazoned with an etching of the wingless dragon.

"What am I doing to draw this kind of magic?" Lia asked.

"Sharing yourself, connecting your essence, don't you see? A rock can go through eternity without a thought, but if inspired with the right spirit, it comes alive. And in some cases it'll attach itself t'that one special soul."

He winked at her before continuing, "Those crystals were given eons of devotion by skilled dwarfs. They empowered them t'greatness the likes we've yet t'see again. Something about you awakened one back t'life. That's why even the wee version you carry is such a treasure."

"But what about the quartz here in the courtyard? They look as big, as beautiful as the ones back home."

"Big and beautiful, yes. Capable of power, yes. We use them

t'shine up our metals, enhance our food and drink, even to swirl up curtains of mist t'hide passage into r'caves. But they're babes really, and don't hold a torch t'the ones in your village. Takes time t'build such power." Laguz eyed Lia. "Time or a whole lot of magic beyond my understanding."

The elder dwarf suddenly scurried away and retrieved a handsome sword leaning against the table. "Here now, I'll show you the difference. This blade was kissed by one o'these crystals. Wynn, would you do the honor of cutting this here bench?"

Wynn's brow shot up, but he took the blade and swiped it hard against the wood. It cut through nearly half the width of the bench seat. They all nodded in appreciation.

"Now take your sword and do the same."

Wynn set the other blade down and unsheathed his own. His sword flashed with light and he swung it down onto another section of the bench, cutting it clean through. "Incredible!"

"And honorable. Your blade will know your intention from the moment you touch it, so no worries over slicing the wrong target."

"I had no idea the crystals were so . . ." Lia trailed.

"Vital? Eminent?" the dwarf finished.

Lia winced at his words and sighed. "How you must hate us. Our people, they robbed the crystals from you, then drove you away."

"Simply the changing of the tides; you get used t'it when you live as long as we do. Our race has seen humankind's dawn and we'll be here t'see its dusk. Child, I'd never hate you, but I am worried 'bout what's t'come. Those quartz towers were enchanted with a special magic. Every dwarf clan existing at the time rallied together with our high sages, all pouring from their hearts and souls into the stones, imbuing into them an important purpose. A purpose carried out even now."

"Now? But, I thought they'd gone to sleep, nobody caring for them and all?"

"Well, they're kinda like a sleeping mother, one eye always open. But you have a point, and that's part of what we need t'know. How much longer will the magic last? How much longer can they enchant the veil?"

"The veil?" Lia's brow drew together.

"Brume's fog, child, the veil between our worlds, the great crystal guardians dotting the hills of your village hold and keep the wall of fog. Over the past century, we've sensed a shift, and we're all wondering what it means."

An unfriendly voice cut in, "Yes, and I'd think the clan chief, even our high king, might want to be to hear the answer to our most important question, don't you agree?"

Lia spun around to see the clan sage behind them, his face twisted in malice.

"Schorl, just helping our fine friends understand a bit about the stones." Laguz turned toward the clan sage and Lia shoved her crystal back into its pouch.

149

Schorl's eyes moved from Wynn's bright sword to the glowing shield, and then to the broken bench. "Been busy, I see. Perhaps you can tear yourselves away to meet with the chief?"

Lia's stomach flipped in alarm. She hoped the chief didn't hate humans as Schorl obviously did. Perhaps he was more like Gobann and Laguz, friendly and grudgeless.

"Schorl, sir, I know how you must feel," she began. "Our ancestors were cruel for driving away the dwarf race, but some of us are different. Some of us still honor the workings of nature, of magic, and only wish for—"

Schorl let out a mirthless laugh, the braids of his beard jostling like snakes against his chin. "Foolish, foolish child. You know nothing of what I feel. How could you possibly, filthy human that you are?" He let out more haughty chuckles while he shook his head.

Wynn stepped forward with his blade in hand. "I don't care who you are, clan sage or not, you're nothing but a fat stump. Talk that way to my cousin again and I'll split you in half like this bench."

A flash of fear crossed Schorl's face. His eyes held firm on the enchanted blade. One flick of it from Wynn, one moment's intention, and the dwarf would be dead. Schorl screwed up his lips, struggling for words, but found none.

"Well now, looks like a simple misunderstanding, eh?" Laguz said. "We're all here trying to help our own, and all have noble reasons. Don't see why we can't help each other peacefully. 'Sides, Wynn, you've never feasted at a dwarf's supper. I say we all greet our

150

chief and enjoy some grub. That all right with you, Schorl?"

The clan sage nodded, his face grown pallid.

Lia's eyes flickered over Schorl. He displayed no wisdom, nor voice of reason for the greater good. The dwarf sage acted no different from the royal sages of Nemetona, and Lia feared his wrath against them would not assuage easily.

Three armored guards ambled forward then, heads down and grumbling until they spotted Wynn's blade. They halted at once, nearly tripping over each other.

"Escort them to the dining hall," Schorl uttered through his teeth.

The guards hesitated, and Laguz motioned for Wynn to sheath the sword. "Please, no need t'wield it; by my word they'll not touch either of you."

Lia and Wynn were led back into the tunnel. The two guards behind them kept a healthy distance. They wended through endless passages until Lia thought they might be heading into the very bowels of the earth. While her body trudged along, her mind spun with all that she'd learned. Her quartz talisman had revealed itself. And its revelations stunned her.

Rockberg's crystals hold and keep the wall of fog. Like sentries at a castle's gates, the stones were in charge of the misty barrier. *Sentries! Of course. By the light of a sentry stone—another part of the elixir revealed.*

She pulled her cloak tighter about her shoulders, wondering how anyone could live underground. She wiped at the dampness on her face. Then a sudden dread crept within her. The *Luis* tree wyrm had warned them, "The guardians are losing power. Darkness devours the veil."

Lia shuddered at the memory of those ink black images, the horrid whispers, the laughter. Laguz was right to worry. The guardian stones were weakening, and giving way to the power of the shades.

Keys

The monotonous thumping of miners' picks grew louder and Lia wondered how close they were to *Duir's Run*. Destiny pushed them closer to the clan chief, and the urge to seek out the portal and flee gripped her insides.

She sucked in the damp air. *Just a little longer, a little more time in these dark tunnels. The least we can do to repay Laguz's help is to share supper with the chief and answer whatever questions we can.*

"In here," the lead guard said, waving them through a doorway tall enough for Wynn.

Lia entered and her eyes grew wide. An enormous cavern sprawled in front of her, fluttering with activity. A table of gigantic proportions sat in the center of the room, surrounded by at least thirty high-backed chairs. The head of the table boasted the largest chair—a throne cushioned in red velvet with arms carved into the shape of claws.

Lia smoothed her hand over the polished wood of the table. Da would appreciate the craftsmanship. Her chest tightened. *Just a little longer, Da. Soon, you'll be back in your woodshop creating another masterpiece.*

She swallowed over the lump in her throat and lifted her eyes to the grand walls. Swords and battle-axes hung alongside tapestries embroidered in silk. Some of the tapestries depicted landscapes of snowy mountains, but the finest of them hung behind the chief's throne. The same wingless dragon etched on the dwarfs' armor embellished the heavy cloth.

Lia stepped closer to admire its detail. The dragon's white scales shone in the torchlight, as did its blue eyes. It stood upon two enormous claws and a tail that stretched like a serpent behind it. Spines ran from snout to tail, rows of teeth lined its half-opened mouth, and a set of horns jutted skyward. Lia wondered if the *Luis* tree wyrm had any relation to the beast.

She recalled the only verse in the *Grimoire* that spoke of these creatures:

> *Wings or feet and colors of any,*
> *The races of dragons are many;*
> *Young or old they are all the same:*
> *They all hoard treasure and guard it with flame.*

She moved aside when a handful of dwarfs scurried to cover the table with platters. She'd never seen so much food all at once: roasted pheasant, fried trout, stewed venison, an entire boar covered with sliced apples, skewers of fired vegetables, sweetmeats, honey cakes, and pitchers of frothy ale to wash it down. Then her eye caught the sparkles. She peered at the dishes to find gemstones sprinkled like salt on all of them.

"Come, come, you will sit across from your kinsman. Guests sit near the head, but not directly at the chief's side." The hostess dwarf from ealier pushed Lia to a chair directly across the table from Wynn. The dwarf's beard danced with pink and yellow stones as she moved to fill a mug and place it in front of Lia.

Lia peered at the ale, leery to drink it lest it contained more woozy brew.

"You've the honor of sitting next to the chief's wife, Lady Othila," the dwarf chirped at her, and then pointed at Wynn. "Lad, you'll have Gobann on your right, since he brought you to us, and Laguz will sit to your left. Of course our clan sage and captain of the guard always sit directly on either side of the chief."

Wynn eyed the dwarf as if she'd sprouted horns. Lia wished they didn't have so much table between them, so they could talk without prying ears.

An entourage of dwarfs suddenly spilled into the room, filling the dining chairs with a furor. Every dwarf wore a beard ranging in various hues and all the women's beards shone with gemstones. Lia winced at the rise of voices. She shifted in her seat as numerous faces turned toward her. Anger flashed across their eyes, and her gut twisted in warning.

Laguz will arrive soon, she told herself. *Perhaps then, they'll realize we aren't all bad.*

A dwarf with timeworn skin and thinning hair crept up to the chair on Lia's left. He leaned his gnarled walking staff against the table and fixed his eyes on her. "Y'look like your kinswoman, hair like a drake's fire, though she was much younger when we met. Name's Haegl, and y'must be Lia, bearer of the quartz."

"Haegl . . . oh yes! You're the retired scout who met our grandma." Lia glanced toward Wynn to get his attention, but Gobann was greeting him. The friendly dwarf patted him on the shoulder, though the gesture failed to ease Wynn's iron posture.

Haegl eased his creaking body onto the chair and spoke to Lia in a low voice, "Maze skipper, she was. I always wondered how she got through the fog's labyrinth. When I asked her about it, she said her friends let her through. 'What friends?' I asked her, but she never answered. 'Tis a mystery perhaps y'can solve for me now, seeing as ye've followed in her footsteps."

Lia's stomach tightened. "Uh, well, we used her amber . . ." Her words trailed. She thought of the shades' false friendship and grappled with how much of the truth she should reveal to Haegl before speaking further with Laguz.

"Ah, she showed me her resin stone," he said, nodding. "Said it was all she had of her mother."

Her mother? Lia swiveled her head around to meet Haegl's deep-set eyes, banishing all other sounds from the room. "What else did she say?"

"Not what she said really, but more what she wore that confounded me." He drank from his mug, coating his beard with froth. "Said that was all she had of her father—a fine mantle of the deepest blue. She had it on inside out, and when I asked her why, she screwed up her face and seemed to think hard about answering me. Then she tossed it off and put it right, and that's when I saw it."

"Saw what?" Lia pressed.

"The royal crest. A fine display of a long bow set with an arrow, entwined in ivy, and aimed toward the sky."

"Her father's mantle bore Nemetona's crest?" Her voice carried across the table.

"Lee, what's going on?" Wynn's brow creased and all but Gobann and Haegl glared at her.

She started to reply, but clamped her mouth shut at the sight of Schorl and a dwarf with burly muscles tromping to their designated seats. Laguz hurried in, planting himself between Wynn and the scowling clan sage. The crystallographer looked as if he'd come out of a windstorm. His white hair stood on end and his spectacles hung askew. Lia tried to catch his attention, but he was too busy fidgeting with his chair to notice her.

The captain of the guard sat with a thunk to the left of the chief's chair, leaving a single empty seat between himself and Lia. He gave her a single nod and she returned it with a nervous smile.

Just as Lia started to turn back to Haegl, the clan chief and his lady sauntered into the room. With a resounding grunt, the dwarfs bellowed a unified greeting for their ruler. Like a fiery mountain, the chief was rock-solid with red hair and a beard to match. Donned in a woolen robe the color of rubies, the chief paled everyone else in the room. He wore no crown, but instead thick golden chains wove around his neck and a huge emerald glimmered against his chest.

"My beautiful wife, Lady Othila," he announced with a wink.

The dwarfs cheered as the yellow haired and bearded chief's wife made her place between the captain and Lia. She took her seat and whispered to Lia, "You and I must speak alone after."

Lia stilled. No greeting, no formalities, only a hushed request to speak in private. Her breath turned shallow. Her circumstances pressed against her: the dank caverns, the dwarfs' anger, the insights about her quartz, Grandma's mantle, and now the chief's wife.

"Welcome, young guests. Not since your two elders have we seen your kind roaming our lands." The chief's booming voice echoed off the walls. The other dwarfs responded with nods and grunts. "Schorl tells me you harbor a bit of the ancient quartz, and Laguz says it responds to you. So tell me, Lia of the human lands, how did you come upon a piece from our unbreakable stones?"

Lia's face burned under the chief's eyes, his face a mix of merriment and supremacy. She rallied her courage. "With respect, I don't know how the crystal broke free. I've never seen pieces cast off before."

The room filled with whispers. She swallowed hard, her eyes

darting between Wynn and the chief. "You see, my garden's in the shape of a spiral with one of the quartz towers at its center. I thought the sun's reflection off it might be good for the plants, those facets so brilliant in the light. My hound actually found the quartz piece. He brought it to me while I was harvesting sticklewort."

The room went silent. Then the chief's laughter roared across the table. His mouth gaped with cheer, but his eyes remained hard as granite.

"Well now, you make it sound like one of our sacred stones cast off a piece to some hairy mutt. Perhaps this beast of yours can tell us how he did it, eh?" Nervous laughter slipped from a few mouths and Lia noticed Schorl smirking at her. With a sinking feeling, Lia averted her eyes.

"More of this later, for now we feast." The chief proceeded to stuff chunks of dripping meat into his mouth, each bite adorned with diamonds.

Lia's stomach churned, though more from worry than the king's diet. She picked at her plate to give the illusion of eating. Nerves gripped her body and her eyes fell on Wynn, her only comfort in the room. He matched her gaze with a tight jaw and lines etched in his forehead. She could hardly think, pinned on one side by the old scout whose words confused her and on the other side by Lady Othila eager for her ear. Schorl captured the chief's attention. The clan sage was leaned over, whispering to his ruler.

"Excuse me, but I need to use the privy." Lia rose from her

chair. Wynn's eyes followed her and she nodded in an effort to reassure him. She tried to avoid the looks of disdain shooting at her, but she couldn't ignore the audible hiss, "Thief!" as she approached the door.

A guard promptly escorted Lia to a room at the end of a narrow hall. A torch burned within, its smoke curling like a snake up a ventilation shaft. In the far corner stretched a stone bench with a hole. Though the room was tiny and dank, she welcomed the solitude.

Wynn had been right from the start, she thought. Gobann meant well, and certainly Laguz, but there were many dwarfs within the chilly caves simmering in bitter memories. Her claim to a piece of their ancient quartz sparked fire on age-old tinder. If Haegl's discoveries about Grandma were known, they'd believe she and Wynn had ties to Nemetona's monarchy, adding to their scorn. Haegl'd been mistaken, of course. The design on Grandma's mantle must've only resembled the true crest. Perhaps one of the old widows embroidered a fanciful emblem to please Grandma.

The low drone of hammers echoed through the thick stone. Lia supposed the majority of dwarfs were kind-hearted, tending to their crafts and family, uninterested in the workings of power. That seemed to be the way of it in most lands, a few power-mongers ruling over the populace.

Her leather pouch hung like a noose around her neck, the quartz weighing heavier by the minute. Yet the thought of losing it gripped her core. She grasped the pouch and the stone's heat answered her touch, reminding her that it was her talisman. It was also a piece of home, of her garden, a reminder of Koun, and a powerful key to the old ways.

She tucked the pouch under her tunic, close to her heart, and returned to the dining room entrance only to be pushed back into the hall.

"M'Lady Othila wishes a word." The guard grabbed Lia's elbow and led her to an adjacent room.

Her pulse raced as the guard pushed her inside a chamber and closed the door. Lia blinked in the lavish room. A candelabrum hung from the ceiling, colored silks lined the walls, and a white fur adorned the floor. In the center, Othila sat on a plush bench sipping from a goblet. "Please sit; have some wine."

Lia eased onto the opposite bench, ignoring the goblet of wine and platter of sweetmeats on the small table between them.

Othila peered at her for a moment, and then blurted, "I want to have a baby, and you shall help me."

"Oh," Lia stammered, "I, uh, don't understand."

"With the quartz, you can charm my womb." An embittered smile crossed Othila's face. "Dwarf women rarely bear younglings. We live hundreds of years, but only one in about fifty of our women ever bear offspring, and then never more than one. Perhaps it's nature's way of keeping us in balance. But if I don't have the chief's heir, he'll be forced to take the next arranged wife. I'm his twelfth already. I'll be reduced to answering to his new bride, no longer his mate, yet unable to marry again."

Othila's eyes welled up and sympathy replaced Lia's fear. Arranged marriages, pressure to provide heirs, abandonment or worse if you didn't birth sons, all typical injustices suffered by women of high titles. Lia would take peasantry and the freedom to choose her mate over all the pomp and finery in the world.

Kelven spilled into her thoughts and she warmed at the memory of his confession. He'd felt the same about her, had for years. Their moment of sweetness was over too fast, but soon, she hoped, they'd be together again.

Lia released the quartz from its pouch. "I shall try, though I can't promise—"

"I know you can do it. Laguz says you are a wonder, power flowing through you akin to the highest sages. Rare are those who connect with such ease to the stones." Tears glistened like dew on Othila's face.

Lia flushed at such a comparison, unsure how to respond beyond a nod. She took a deep breath and closed her eyes. Devotion for her stone filled her. She sent her mind outward, just as Laguz had shown her, focusing her thoughts deep within the crystal.

She drew from her memory all the living creatures she had ever nurtured. She recalled tending to baby birds fallen from their nests, her countless honeybees, an injured fox, their horses, and of course her hound, Koun. Her love for all of them flowed within her, and she implored the quartz to help Othila.

The crystal's heat grew, nearly scorching Lia's palm, and she opened her eyes to the light expanding from it. Her heart raced. She was doing it, wielding the crystal all on her own. Her talisman was answering her call.

Holding onto to her connection, she rose from her bench and sat next to Othila. She placed her free palm down on Othila's belly, feeling the woman twitch.

"Your hand," Othila murmured, "so hot, and the light . . ."

After a few moments the flow of energy ebbed, the quartz grew cool, and Lia withdrew her hand and tucked the stone away. "That's as much as I can do."

"I cannot thank you enough." Othila clasped Lia's hands into her own. "Forgive me, but I had to wait until after your charm was complete to tell you, for only magic from an untroubled heart could ever inspire new life."

Prickles of warning ran up Lia's spine. "Tell me what?"

Othila continued, "My husband is a good ruler, who wishes only to protect his clan, but Schorl claims his loyalty and he's convinced him to keep you here. Schorl plans to use your connection to the stone, force you to wield magic in order to gain power over the other clans, even the High King. That is until he figures out a way to sever the stone's bond from you and take it for himself."

Panic gripped Lia. "I must get to Wynn. How do we escape? Can Gobann help us or Laguz—?"

163

Othila help up her hand to quiet Lia. "I've made arrangements. But I'm sorry to tell you, Laguz has been banished. Schorl sent him to our isolation caves, though he's sure to bring him back soon. Crystalography is a treasurered skill after all."

Schorl's the one who should be thrown in those caves!

"Othila, you must find a way to get word to Laguz. He was right—the crystals' enchantment wanes. Dark powers consume Brume's fog."

"We've wondered as much," she said. "That fog was meant to remain a labyrinth, a maze to fool the traveler, assuring he always ended up right back where he started, never harmed, never killed, for we truly are a peaceful race."

Her eyes met Lia's. "It was your kinswoman who told Haegl that people died in the fog, and that she gained special passage by bringing gifts to its guards. Her friends, she called them. Our scout knew nothing of deaths or guards, figured something had gone terribly wrong, and pressed her for more, but she fled from him scared. She eluded him from then on, as did your kinsman, for they mostly stayed within the boundaries of the fae meadow where we dwarfs do not cross."

A light tapping on the door jolted Lia from Othila's words. Wynn and Gobann slipped inside the room, and relief swept through Lia.

Othila stood. "Is everyone in place?"

"Aye, M'Lady, they're all headed t'the meeting room now,

'specting your guards t'bring our guests down shortly. They'll be mighty surprised when they don't show."

"I'll handle them; you just get our friends back safe." Othila turned her eyes on Lia and placed a hand on her shoulder. "You, my dear, shall be fondly remembered."

"And you as well," Lia replied.

With those parting words, Lia and Wynn followed Gobann out the door. The clanking of dishes and the low hum of voices carried from the dining hall, and Gobann rushed them across the tunnel and through a stout door.

"Stay close and quiet," Gobann said.

They hurried through a series of passages, some lit by torches, others so dark they had to link hands. Despite the chilled air, sweat beaded across Lia's brow. All their hopes hung beyond the walls of the icy caverns.

They ran for what seemed like an eternity through the tunnels with only the sounds of their labored breath accompanying them. Lia kept glancing back for signs of pursuit. When they turned down a hall where voices echoed, Gobann ushered them into a dark chamber.

"Miners," Gobann uttered when the passage grew silent again. "'Tis all that's down in these parts. 'Fraid I had t'take you the long way round, else we'd never make it without being seen."

The dwarf scout waved them on, moving deftly through the shadows like a lynx. The walls turned slick with water and puddles covered the ground. The knocking of miners' picks grew and Lia's heart drummed in answer. She trudged through the dark and dared to think of soil and sky.

She chanted to herself, "Almost there," scurrying through tunnel after tunnel, with hammers echoing through her ears, thoughts pounding in her head, until they were once again running through *Duir's Run*, and back in the green foothills of Brume.

Whorl

ere we are, back in the lowlands." Gobann drew back his woolen hood. "You've plenty o'time t'run. Othila's a clever one; she'll have them fooled for a while t'be sure. You've the night on your side, and once you head upriver and get across, they'll not follow. Dwarfs aren't much for riding boats or beasts and we can't swim worth a lick."

Wynn reached his hand out and patted Gobann on the shoulder. "Thanks for helping us."

"'Tis a shame it didn't work out better. Guess I 'spected too much, lowly scout and all. Sorry I couldn't get you that new sword, young warrior, but I be thinking you're probably better off with the one you got." Gobann winked.

The dwarf shifted his eyes onto Lia and she warmed in the pools of kindness. "Many thanks, Gobann. I know you meant well, and if you hadn't taken us in, I wouldn't have learned what the crystal could do."

"Ah, you would have figur'd it out eventually. You've the touch. Oh, almost forgot this for the lad." Gobann pulled back his cloak to reveal the shield charmed by Lia's stone. It sparkled under the moonlight, the wingless dragon ethereal on its front. "A right shield t'match your sword. Laguz made sure you got it. That lindwyrm'll keep you safe."

Wynn's face lit up, his eyes roving across the etching. "Lindwyrm?"

"Lindwyrm dragon. Their kind live deep in the mountain caves. Only saw one m'whole life, skin pale as bone and eyes like fire opals. But like with any drake, you never get too friendly."

Gobann donned his cloak. "One more thing before I get on, a swig or two of the silver waters is all right, but 'tis best not t'fish from the Seren River. Enchanted waters poured straight from the heart o'Brume. Life's special, sacred within them. Farewell to you now."

"Wait, what about our horses?" Lia blurted.

Gobann let out a chuckle. "Almost forgot."

He whistled loudly and after a few moments, the ivory horse galloped up the hill, followed by Merrie and Nolan. Gypsum walked to Gobann's side. The dwarf murmured something into her ear, and then he turned back to Lia and Wynn. "She'll guide you upriver to the *Coll* grove. Farewell friends."

"Farewell," Lia and Wynn said in unison, and Gobann disappeared back into *Duir's Run*.

"So we're headed to a *Coll* grove?" Wynn asked, stroking Nolan's muzzle.

"Yes, hazel trees." Lia rubbed her face against Merrie's soft coat, breathing in the familiar smell. Some of the knots unraveled within her. "It'll take us the rest of the night to get there. We can cross the river at sunrise."

She mounted Merrie and imparted a farewell to the *Duir* tree. She'd always admire its magic portal, though she was much relieved to be leaving it. "You were right all along, Wynn. We could have been trapped in those caves forever—"

"We're back, we're all right, and you learned how to wield your stone." He smiled. "And I've a sword and shield like no other."

She gave him a nod and they sped up the hills, putting plenty of distance between themselves and the dwarfs' doorway into the valleyland before they slowed their pace. A clear night sky stretched overhead and the swollen moon offered a beacon to light their way.

"Easy, boy," Wynn soothed, trying to keep Nolan from nipping at Gypsum's backside. "For a gelding, he's certainly taken by her."

"Hmm," Lia agreed. The strange horse cantered in silence, featherlike across the terrain. Her silken tail nearly swept the ground and her coat shined in pearly perfection. She was a beast unlike any from Nemetona or possibly anywhere else but Brume.

Wynn steadied Nolan's pace to match Merrie's. "What happened between you and the chief's wife?"

"Would you believe she asked me to use the stone on her womb? Guess dwarfs have a bit of trouble making younglings. The strangest part, though, was I think it worked."

"Huh. Explains why she was so helpful."

"I will always be grateful for her kindness, for Gobann's help, and for all that Laguz taught me." Lia folded her hand around her pouch. The quartz within warmed to her touch, ready to do her bidding.

"Yeah," Wynn replied. "Those three helped offset that vermin, Schorl, and his puppet chief. Especially Laguz. My da's going to swallow his pipe when he sees my new blade."

Thoughts about all that had happened inside the dwarfs' caves wove like ribbons through Lia's mind. Her discoveries were priceless, even the frightening ones. The most disturbing revelation was the dark fate of Brume's fog. Like a beast crawling with mites, it suffered an infestation of shades. To what end they devoured the veil was a mystery, but one thing was certain: the shades would continue to grow in power and tear to shreds anyone in their way.

Unless the great crystals' magic returned to full power. But how?

Her thoughts shifted to another nagging discovery: the crest embroidered on Grandma's cloak. As much as she reasoned that the design was the fanciful stitchings of an old mountain widow, she couldn't shake the certainty in Haegl's voice. And if it was a fanciful adornment, then why did Grandma hide it by wearing the mantle inside out?

Like the horses' footfalls up the steepening terrain, Lia's thoughts never ceased. After hours of travel, her head hung in weariness and her stomach grumbled. *Keep going, keep moving,* she commanded herself, but the growing rush of streams beckoned to her and she finally gave in to her body. "Wynn, let's stop for a rest, catch some food."

Wynn hesitated. "All right, we've covered enough ground for now."

They heeded Gobann's warning, making sure the stream ran from the opposite direction of the Seren River. Lia retrieved two of Kelven's carved spears, handing one to Wynn. They edged the stream and Lia peered into the bubbling waters.

"Wish we had that undine faery to corral us some fish," Lia said.

"Don't need her!" Wynn drew up a healthy trout. "Barely saw the thing, jabbed down once, and there it was. Look at the size of him."

Lia gaped at it. Before she could reply, Wynn speared a second fish. "Did you see that? That trout came out of the water, like it wanted me to spear it." He continued stalking the stream and within minutes skewered five trout in total.

Lia cleaned the fish, perplexed by their speedy capture, while Wynn built a fire. He gathered firewood from the blanket of golden gorse, or *Onn* shrubs, covering the highlands. The low shrubs provided a windbreak and their wood burned fiercely hot.

171

As Lia strung the last trout, she spotted a trail of gold on the water. It rippled by her like a strand of thread. *What magic is this?* The stream didn't flow from the Seren River, and the trail shone gold rather than silver besides, but magic of some sort created it.

A luminescent glow caught the corner of Lia's eye. She peered upstream to its source and froze in shock. Gypsum's muzzle aimed down to the stream's edge. A beacon of gold light protruded from her forehead to pierce the waters below.

"She's a unicorn!"

Wynn scrambled from the fire and gawked at Gypsum. "A unicorn? But I don't see a horn."

Gypsum tossed her head, fixed her indigo eyes on Lia, and then pranced toward Merrie and Nolan.

Lia could barely speak. "Her horn reached into the stream . . . a spiral of gold."

"Here let me take those." Wynn grabbed hold of the strung fish nearly falling from Lia's hand. "Guess it wasn't my fishing skills that got us all this trout. Sure wish I could see her horn, but then I don't have your special sight."

"No, it's not because of special sight, Wynn; it's because of my maidenhood." Lia sucked in cool air before reciting a verse from the *Grimoire*,

> *Unicorn of silver sheen,*
> *Pure as winter's snow;*
> *By maiden's eyes you can be seen,*
> *Under a moon's midnight glow.*

ARROW OF THE MIST

Wynn gave her an awkward grin. Then his brow rose at Nolan's frolicking close to Gypsum. "Poor guy doesn't stand a chance. Though, I can't blame him for trying."

Lia noticed that even Merrie edged closer to the unicorn.

Lia's stomach grumbled and she returned her focus to the fish. She seasoned them with thyme and sage, and then fried them to a succulent finish. She rubbed the last of their vegetables with the same herbs and skewered them over the flames. Warmed by food and fire, Lia and Wynn allowed themselves a moment's rest.

"Let's see, faeries, a rock giant, ballybogs, dwarfs, and now a unicorn," Wynn said. "Kinda makes you wonder what's next."

"I'd say Brume's a bit more than deadly sea cliffs and barren knife-edged mountains," Lia said. "Never could understand how our rulers got away with imposing that notion. None of them ever came through the fog. And the people go along with it."

"It's simple, really. Not many rulers want to share power with the unknown, or even worse, compete with a bunch of legends. So they cleverly explain them away, force their will through laws and punishment, until everyone follows their word."

"Just like Schorl, only interested in his own personal gain." Lia used her fingers to comb through her hair. "Figured it'd be different with dwarf rulers."

"Power is power. But it turned out all right. Like you said, you learned about your stone." Wynn gathered up their dishes and headed toward the stream to rinse them.

Lia grabbed her knapsack and began tossing items out. She sorted through the pouches, setting some aside and returning others, until she sat before an organized collection.

"What are you doing?" Wynn asked, returning to the fire.

"For the elixir. The riddle calls for three parts herb. Here's lion's tooth, grass of goose, and after some thought, I've decided on quitch grass. It cleans the blood and soothes the insides." Lia laid the plant parts out in order. "There's two parts tree, so here's the *Nion* and *Saille*, and a snippet of golden bough."

"You've almost got it," Wynn said. "Six plants and you said yourself that you're a maiden. That makes seven out of thirteen parts. What's left?"

"The enemy—a plant of a different nature." A chill crawled up Lia's back at the thought of harvesting a piece of the *Straif.* "Then four things I don't know yet: alicorn, Brume's blood, mother, and crone. Thanks to Laguz I figured out the sentry stone part." Lia pulled out her quartz pouch and dangled it gently.

"Ah, makes sense," Wynn said. "But I never would have thought it were those big old rocks holding up that wall of fog. Guess I shouldn't call them rocks anymore."

"Lady Othila told me the fog was enchanted to be a maze, always leading the traveler out from where they came in."

"A maze, huh?" Wynn's brow rose.

"The Scalach shades changed all of that when the crystals' power weakened from neglect. The shades' claim on Brume's fog is getting stronger, and I hate to think what will happen if they gain complete control of it."

"Hmm, I guess even the strongest magic needs upkeep." Wynn nudged closer to the fire. "Maybe everyone should start paying attention to Rockberg's crystals."

Lia agreed, though she doubted the best showerings of attention would bring back the level of magic they needed in time. Like a hole in a fence, the *Straif* had found an opening in the fog, and it was perhaps the first of many.

"You know the way I see it," Wynn said, "is if you're the maiden, then mother and crone must be your elder women kin."

Lia shifted her thoughts back to the elixir. "Well, that would mean my ma, but what about the crone? There's no one to fill her role. It sounds right, but I hope you're wrong."

She tossed the herbs back into her knapsack, her mood turning grim. She forced back the tears that threatened. More than eight days had passed since Da's attack, and six days since the *Straif* attacked Granda. Even with Ebrill's herbs, they suffered while she and Wynn grappled with the riddles of Brume.

"I thought this would help," Lia said. "But it only proves how slim our chances are of carrying it all out. If even one of the thirteen ingredients is missing, the magic of the elixir won't take. And aside from a missing crone and deciphering the other parts, we still have to face the *Straif.*"

Wynn let out his breath. "Well, we're not defenseless. You've got the quartz and I've got my blade and shield. In fact, why not put your little stone to work now? Maybe it can answer some questions."

Lia chewed on her lip. She'd commanded the stone with Laguz and used it to help Othila, but her confidence wavered now that she was away from the dwarfs. Wynn seated himself cross-legged in front her and gave her an encouraging pat. "Just try," he said.

She opened her pouch and tumbled the stone into her palm. The quartz warmed in her hand. Laguz believed in her in ability to wield the quartz, as did all of the dwarfs, even Schorl. Grandma wielded the amber on her own.

It's my turn to take charge of my talisman.

She closed her eyes and focused her mind, connecting, searching, until a fiery heat spread through her. The magic tugged at her, like a rope pulling deep within her belly, drawing from her energy to kindle its power.

Ohhh.

She sucked in air, as if she'd sprinted up a hill. The dwarfs' stone-mage energies must've offset the draw from her body. Perhaps the nearby quartz towers helped feed the little stone. Whatever the reason, she'd have to be careful not to exert herself overmuch while she connected to the magic.

She opened her eyes to a bright light, like an upside down triangle resting on her palm. A stream of images poured into the light: her grandparents harvesting herbs, then back in time to their wedding, and further back to when Grandma dwelt in the Bronach

Mountains. The images came too fast. Lia wished to linger with each one, but the magic had a more important purpose.

The vision flashed to Rockberg where the crystals shot out cords of light, like arms stretched toward the wall of fog, holding it even as their power waned. A chill ran through Lia's bones. Numerous dark figures prowled the fog like bloodthirsty sharks. Even in the vision, the Scalach shades filled her with dread.

The images spun on and Lia flinched at the sound of a woman's scream. At the edge of the fog in a cool pine, or *Ailm* forest, huddled a woman with a crown of red hair. Her crumpled body shook violently on the ground, her moans of agony echoing through the murk. The woman clawed at her naked, swollen belly. She scratched into her woad-dyed flesh, turning the blue tattoos to purple. All at once, the raging river within her burst free, and from the fierce and fatal gush of blood, mewled the thin cry of a babe.

The scene promptly shifted and Lia's already racing heart skipped. Two crones with faces drawn and pale stumbled toward the infant's wails. Then clips of pictures flashed: the babe washed and swaddled; the mother's dead body stripped, her indelible markings rubbed with oils; a flurry within the fog above, as if the misty vapors fought in some eerie battle. Then the vision skipped ahead.

A fresh grave emerged, its soil caressed by the fog. The first crone set fire to a bundle of sage. The smoke billowed over the buried remains. She chanted the same mysterious words over and over, the incantation echoing in Lia's mind, and then she threw an

assortment of fresh herbs over the mound. Lia recognized a few—
Ailm needles, dew of the sea, muggons, candlewick—and she stored
the others in memory to decipher later.

In a great windy upsurge, the wraiths hovering at the edge of the
fog fled. The mother's soul flew like a silver ribbon from the shades'
desperate clutches. The crone's burial rites had set the woman's spirit
free.

The second crone remained standing with her eyes closed, soft
whispers spilling from thin lips. She cradled the babe in the nook of
her bony arm, the swaddling cloth made of the finest blue velvet.

"Her mother's amber, something to give her in time," the first
crone crackled, settling the sunny stone within the folds of velvet.
"Made off with Gorsedd's mantle, I see. Didn't know what he was in
for with the likes a'her. Not even a king can tame one from the
tribes."

"Best t'keep the babe hidden for a while, away from those
soldiers' prying eyes. King'll give up soon I 'spect, get back to his
posh castle, find and marry some docile wench," the second crone
rattled, shifting the babe forward, and then she stepped to the edge
of the grave. "Your mum's free now, lass, but you've a strange fate.
You've the fog in your lungs, your pores soaked in these mists. Born
'tween two worlds, you've drawn peculiar magic from this place, and
I fear it'll call you back someday."

The babe wailed on, her tiny bawl and image fading, and the
quartz grew cool in Lia's hand.

"I, I guess it's done." She closed her fingers over the crystal. "I didn't learn anymore about the elixir, but I saw Grandma Myrna birthed in the fog border. I'd heard about it before, from the *Nion* tree guardian. She said Grandma drew her first breaths from the mists."

She swallowed hard. "Wynn, I watched her mother, our great-grandma, die in labor all alone in that *Ailm* forest. Two old widows found the crying babe and, well—"

Lia paused, trying to sort out her amazement. She peered at Wynn. He tilted his head and flicked his thumbs against his legs, waiting for her to go on.

"That old dwarf scout, Haegl, the one who met Grandma when she was young, told me the amber stone came from her mother and from her father she inherited a mantle. He said it was stitched with a crest: a long bow, set with an arrow, entwined in ivy, and aimed toward the sky. It didn't make any sense to me, but it's all true according to the vision. King Gorsedd was our kin, Wynn. Which makes King Brennus our . . . cousin."

Wynn's eyes rounded. "That's impossible—the *king*? Who was Grandma's mother, certainly not the queen?"

Lia placed the quartz back into its pouch. "Hardly. Her mother was a woman of the mountain tribes. I saw her woad markings. Not sure how the two of them came together, but they did. The widows buried her mother's body, but kept the amber and the king's crested mantle with the babe. They used magic rites to free the woman's spirit from the shades, and afterwards one of the crones mentioned Grandma's strange fate, being born between two worlds."

Wynn rubbed his face and drew in his breath. "Incredible, and yet I've heard a tale like this."

Lia's breath caught. "What tale?"

"I heard this story once in a southland market. I must've been about eight years old, wandering around while my father haggled away our harvest, and this old man spun off a tale to a circle of children.

"He told of a newly crowned king sailing the seas, eager to explore the coastlands of his fair kingdom. Far to the north, he found a strange woman with hair of fire and skin painted by the sky. She spent her days gathering the sun's fallen tears on the seashore, where the icy waters transformed them into honeyed stones.

"It was all very poetic, as you can tell, and the story went on about how the woman wove magic threads around the king's heart, enchanting him under a love spell. For weeks, he languished under her charm, until she vanished into the misty mountains. And though he married another, and produced an heir, every year from then on he took to the sea to scour the shores for her, until years later the waters took mercy and claimed his tormented soul for good."

Lia sat in disbelief. A common bard recited the story of her great-grandparents. Living so far north and having little interest anyway, she'd only heard the most common tales of Nemetona's monarchy. Perhaps she'd listen more carefully to bards.

"Brennus's father, King Arlan, still reigned when you heard this, right?" she asked.

Wynn nodded.

"I'm surprised that storyteller wasn't hammered on the spot for spinning a yarn about the king's mother's rival."

"I guess even a king can't watch all of the people all of the time," Wynn said. "Never would have thought we'd be tied to royals. Or to those mountain tribes for that matter. Strange combination."

Lia's mind clicked with another revelation. "That verse makes sense now, *Parents gone but never forgot, for they leave a legacy of honeyed drops floating nobly, upon a rich velvet sea.*' It's about her mother's amber and her father's velvet mantle." Then her brow furrowed. "I wonder if Granda knows the truth about our royal lineage."

"Maybe, but I doubt anyone else does, including our mothers. I mean if you were Grandma, would you want to risk having yourself and your children subject to certain death? Even a whiff of that sort of knowledge would invite bloodshed from the ruling class. They'd rather see someone perish before sharing any power, especially with kin from some legendary mistress."

"Hmm." Lia nodded in agreement. "Pretty absurd we're related to that fool Brennus. Guess it's something to laugh about when we're old, huh? I want nothing to do with those pompous dolts anyway."

"I agree," Wynn said. "Let's say we get moving, get to that grove so we can cross the river at first light."

Wynn doused the fire, the blaze hissing its farewell, and they mounted their horses. They followed Gypsum up the gorse-covered hills, keeping with her swift pace. An hour later, Lia spotted the *Coll* grove. Toothy leaves became clearer as they neared the trees. The foliage adorned slender branches shooting up from the base of each tree, giving some of the *Colls* a bush-like appearance. The rush of the Seren River was a welcome lullaby to Lia's ears. A couple of precious hours remained before dawn.

"Here's good," Wynn said. "It'll take those dwarfs the rest of the night and most of tomorrow to make it here on foot, and by then we'll be far from their reach."

They slid off their horses and settled at the edge of the grove. Merrie and Nolan nudged close to their unicorn friend. Lia propped up her knapsack as a pillow and stretched out her sore, exhausted body. With her hair warm across her neck, she buried her face in her ma's woolen cloak and breathed the faint scent of home.

Whether from pure exhaustion, magic from the stone, or the unicorn-inspired trout, Lia slept oceans deep. Her dreams carried her far into the northern horizon, soaring above the snowy peaks where she had a bird's eye view of Brume. A crystalline lake, like a perfect mirror, nestled within the heart of two peaks. Like a great ewer, the lake poured out the sparkling Seren River, and it cascaded down the mountains like a bride's veil.

Lia swooped down for a closer look and followed the banks of the life-giving waters. The river poured swift down the mountainside, curving through the hills and wooded valley, dividing the eastern boundaries from the rest of the land.

She soared across the landscape and saw the *Coll* grove nestled against the riverbank. Farther downstream grew the oaks and beeches, and farther still the waterway twisted west, splitting into streams that fed the fae woods. A giant tree grew on the bank at the river's final twist. The glorious yew, or *Idho,* reached its evergreen branches wildly toward the sky. Its pale brown trunk framed an immense hollow. Lia tried to get a closer look, but she felt a soft nudge, then something warm and wet against her cheek.

Lia opened her eyes to her mare's nose. "Merrie, silly horse."

"Wynn, I had the most remarkable dream—" Her words froze on the air when she realized her cousin was gone.

Crown

ia blinked the sleep from her eyes. The gorse shrubs shone gold in the dawning light with no sign of her cousin or his horse among them. She called out for him several times without result.

She tossed her knapsack and quiver of bolts over her shoulder, grabbed her crossbow and set a bolt in the catch, and then began scouring the area. Dawn brightened into morning by the time she spotted numerous hoof prints in the soil. Nolan's shod hoofs were an easy giveaway, but there were a number like Gypsum's—bigger and more circular, a cross between a horse's and a large stag's.

Too many for one unicorn alone, she thought, *and plenty to entice Wynn's steed.*

"Loyal friend," she murmured, patting Merrie on the neck. Then she galloped her up the hills.

The trail of hoof marks held to the riverbank, which made tracking simple. She paid little attention to the silver waters rushing beside her, glad none of the hoof prints led into the them. The sun rose higher in the sky, and she loosened her cloak and slowed Merrie's pace.

Where have they gone? They can't have gotten far in my short hours of sleep.

She'd figured it had been a simple chase: Nolan gone wild over the enchanted stampede, Wynn galloping his incited horse a ways to let him run off steam, but soon gaining back control.

So, why hasn't Wynn turned him round yet? She pushed her hair behind her ears. *Just a little farther. He has to be near.*

She trotted Merrie up the steepening hills and caught sight of a dense *Tinne* grove. The scarlet berries hung heavy amid the evergreens. And the track marks disappeared into the grove.

"Wynn!" She raced into the cluster of trees, only to stop as Merrie reared back from the prickly leaves. The mare snorted and beat her hoofs, and Lia slid down and pulled her into a small clearing where she could leave her. After forcing her tangled hair into a bodkin, Lia continued to search the thicket on foot.

"Wynn, can you hear me?"

Lia fought through the vast coppice for hours, the many scrambled hoof prints leading everywhere and nowhere. She cried his name repeatedly without result. The *Tinne* branches snagged at her cloak, their sharp fingers scratching against cloth and skin.

"Please, answer me!" Her voice turned hoarse and tears of

frustration welled up.

The grove seemed to grow around her, a never-ending labyrinth that mocked her plight. With blurred eyes, she flailed desperately through the confusing maze of trees. The sun neared its zenith in the dull slate sky, and besides her ragged breaths, Lia heard only the rush of the river. She struggled to the edge of the waters, trudged up and down the bank, finding no sign of her cousin.

A sprinkling of rain made its way to the ground, muddling the already confused pattern of prints. Soon, the persistent drizzle soaked her, and she scrambled through the trees until she lost all sense of direction.

Her cries for Wynn, and her whistles for Merrie vanished on the bitter air. Even the sounds of the river rapids faded to silence. She was utterly lost. Her mind and body limped until she collapsed on all fours. She folded her legs underneath her and wept.

Wynn had disappeared in the quiet of night while she slept like a babe, another of her family victimized by Brume. First Grandma, then Da, then Granda, and now Wynn, all of them fallen to this insatiable land.

Hot tears stained her face. She reached a trembling hand up to one of the *Tinnes* and drew down a cluster of berries. Her eyes roved over the smooth beads the color of blood, and her hand warmed to their touch.

They're warm!

She stared at her palm and chided herself. In all her panic, she'd forgotten to do the one thing that might help her find Wynn: connect with the trees. This was their grove after all, their clustered haven where they ruled as kings under bright thorny crowns.

She scooted closer to the shrub tree and placed her hand on its smooth bark. Its leaves, which had slashed at her flesh before, now tickled her hand. She breathed deeply and reached her thoughts outward. Fiery prods pierced her mind.

No, please! Let me go . . .

She pried her hand from the trunk and tried to disconnect her mind from the tree, but it held her thoughts firm. Then a strange chant droned in her head, "Surrender your crown, surrender your crown."

What crown? Oh, help me!

She ground her teeth against the stabbing assault, grasped her head in misery, all while searching her memory for anything that might save her. Nothing came forth. And the pain increased, as if a band of barbs wrapped around her mind.

She tried to crawl away, only to bump against another tree, and another, the grove's hold on her unyielding. Then she clawed at her knapsack and flung pouches of herbs to the ground. The sight of them merged into one painful blur. Just when she thought she'd go mad from the pain, a page from Grandma's *Grimoire* floated from her memory, clear as if it lay right before her.

On the top of the parchment was a sketch of a holly tree, and below it, a verse:

Tinne *tree, evergreen,*
King of the waning days;
Wearing humble thorns peacefully,
In his fair and enchanted maze.

"Wearing . . . humble thorns . . . peacefully," she stammered, and some of her pain ebbed away.

Lia sucked in air and focused again on the page for answers. Her mind's eye skimmed the uses of its bark and leaves, and the warnings for its deadly berries, and stopped at two more verses.

She pressed her hand to her throbbing temples and recited the first one,

Surrender your fight, give up your woe;
For the true path to light, begins with letting go.

The shock from the verse momentarily halted her struggle against the pain, and a wash of relief flooded her mind.

Ahh, thank the glittering stars!

A dull throb remained as the trees kept their invisible hold, but they had released her from the pain as soon as she surrendered to it. Tears of relief streamed down her face.

Surrender everything, she thought, and she let go of the last vestiges of her struggle. She even ceased her despair for Wynn. It was time for trust, to move beyond urgent needs, beyond useless panic, and beyond her shackles of fear. Wynn had vanished, yes, but there was a way to reclaim him. For in the quiet peace where her mind now lingered, she knew that he had not yet perished.

She focused again on the page hovering in her thoughts. The

second verse read:

> Tinne *tree, I cherish thee,*
> *The one-horned beast seeks your sanctuary;*
> *I sacrifice my crown for just one wish:*
> *A bit of alicorn dust willingly relinquished.*

Alicorn. Lia hesitated for only a moment, and then she reached up and pulled the silver bodkin free. Her cherished hair rolled down her back, warm, familiar. She grabbed her knife and its razor edge blinked in readiness.

With her blade at neck level, she swallowed all pride and sawed at the thick sections of her hair, hacking off the length of the only sort of crown she owned. The red tresses tumbled down around her. Her hand fell limp, her knife dropped loosely from it, and she bent her shorn head low. "Take my sacrifice, and I ask only that you free my cousin. Free Wynn!"

A soft nudge and the sound of nickering came from behind. "Merrie—?" Lia lifted her eyes and gasped.

A unicorn bowed its head and Lia reached for its mane. She ran her fingers through the silken hair and the beast eyed her with wells of blue. Lia's voice came raspy, "Where is he?"

The stunning creature tossed its head and a long golden horn flashed into view. It touched its horn to the top of Lia's head. Her scalp tingled in response. Then the unicorn turned and slowly rubbed its horn against the smooth bark of the *Tinne*. With several strokes, a pile of glitter fell from the golden spiral. Lia gazed at the alicorn dust glimmering at the base of the tree and the unicorn backed away. In

189

one final gesture, it bowed before her, and then disappeared into the grove.

"Lee, where are you?"

"Wynn! I'm here." Lia jumped to her feet. Her cousin crashed through the trees and hugged her so tight she had to gasp for air.

"Thank the fallow fields. I thought my mind was lost for good." He released her and rambled on, "We'd barely fallen asleep when all of a sudden I heard them. I looked up and saw Gypsum running with a whole pack of unicorns. Unicorns, Lee, I saw their horns and everything. Then I felt crazed and obsessed, and I jumped on Nolan's back and took chase. I don't understand how, but I think I was under some kind of trance. I couldn't stop; all I could think of was catching one of them. My head's been in a muddle until a second ago. Then all at once it cleared, and I saw you through the trees."

"I was so scared, Wynn. I thought you were gone forever, and then that unicorn came—"

"Your hair," he blurted.

Lia grabbed at her short locks. They felt foreign, as if belonging to someone else. Her eyes lowered to the pile of hair, the ends of the strands still curled like a babe's at the tips. She bit her lip and grasped one of her waist pouches. She bent down to the base of the tree and used her knife to scoop up the pile of glittery substance.

"I did it for the alicorn." *And in exchange for your life*, she kept to herself. "It's unicorn horn dust."

Wynn smiled and squeezed her shoulder. "I knew you'd figure it out. Strange trade, though."

Yes, she thought, *it certainly was.*

Lia gathered her knapsack contents and the duo departed the *Tinne* grove, finding an easy passage out. It was as if the trees had pulled their branches inward to let them pass. Birdsong and the rush of the river replaced the eerie silence from before, and they fetched Merrie and Nolan huddled in the clearing.

Lia reached out with her mind to give thanks to the *Tinnes*. She knew this time there'd be no pain, no lessons, no sacrifice. She'd proven herself well enough and departed with the gifts to show for it.

She respected the *Tinnes'* magic, however difficult it proved to be. Never again would she hear the name of Wynn's little sister, Holly, without thinking of the grove. But unlike the holly trees, her eleven-year-old cousin was gentle and kind, traits more akin to the enchanted beasts that dwelt there.

They rode down the hills and Lia was certain that Nolan pouted for Gypsum. His head drooped and he distanced his muzzle from Merrie. Like threads of moonlight, unicorn magic could be fondly admired, but never captured. However, Gypsum's mystique would linger within each of their memories forever.

"How close do you think they are—the dwarfs I mean?" Lia glanced up at the midday sky.

"I'd guess a few hours. The river crossing's just ahead, and once we're on the other side, we're safe, at least from dwarfs."

"I'm gonna refresh a bit then." Lia veered Merrie to a grassy patch along the river's edge. She left her there and edged the waters, peering into the liquid mirror. Ma would pale at the sight of her. Lia's crowning glory, her long coppery mane, was chopped away.

She dipped her head in the cool river. The waters poured over her like a healing balm, washing away dried tears, soothing her nicks and scratches. She took a deep drink before she lifted back up.

Wynn's jaw dropped and he pointed at her head.

"What's wrong?" A jolt of worry shot through her.

He stammered, "It's, uh, all silver."

Confused, she bent again to look at her reflection. What was left of her hair now matched the color of the river. Lia immediately jumped up and grabbed one of Wynn's skins containing ordinary water.

"Maybe it just coated it." She poured the water over her head and rubbed it vigorously.

Wynn shook his head, his brows pulling downward. "It's still there, but I don't understand. Why doesn't the water stick to our skin or color the horses' muzzles?" Before Lia could respond, Wynn dunked his head under the water. He rose back up with his blond locks dripping, but still yellow.

Lia's stomach knotted. She reflected back to the only explanation—the touch of the unicorn's horn. Her whole scalp had tingled. Brume's waters must've responded to the alicorn residue.

She swallowed over the stone forming in her throat. She cared nothing for fancy clothes, adorning trinkets, or face paints, but she loved her hair. Now hacked away and dyed silver, her blazing tresses were transformed into something odd and garish.

"Maybe the color'll wear off. Or I'm sure it'll grow back in normal," Wynn offered.

Lia mounted Merrie, swallowing tears for her one vanity. It was fodder for more ridicule, she figured, and then she thought of Kelven. What would he think of Wynn's fiery cousin now?

"Nothing I can do about it. Let's go." Lia gritted her teeth and rode down the hill as if she were a soldier in a shining helmet.

They sped back to the *Coll* grove and Lia spotted a wild *Quert* tree tucked at the edge of the wood. The knots in her stomach hid her hunger, but she knew they hadn't eaten since the trout and their food stores were gone.

She approached the tree, motioning for Wynn to wait, and placed her hand on the gnarled trunk. The tree answered her touch, filling her mind with a sense of its bounty, sweet and full, as if she would never feel hunger again.

She tugged at one of the rosy apples, snapped it from its stem, and tossed it toward Wynn. She grabbed one for herself and bit into the crisp, juicy flesh. Her mouth came alive with its sweetness.

"Thiff if the beff apple effer," Wynn mumbled. "But wait: what if they're enchanted?"

"I'm sure they are." Lia continued to chomp away and some of her tension eased. "The tree's roots draw water from the Seren River."

She devoured several more of the fruits, her body energized by the fare, and she gathered a supply to take with them.

"What about the nuts?" Wynn headed into the grove. "Is it all right to gather them, too?"

Lia followed him, leaving their horses to nip at the lush undergrowth. The long branches of the hazel trees entwined together, making it hard to tell where one tree began and the other ended.

She reached out to the *Coll* community, and like a bubbling brook, the trees murmured gentle greetings. Their effervescence tickled her mind, sparking thoughts of all the things she enjoyed: gardening, working beehives, crafting remedies, and studying legends. Muses of the wood, the *Coll* trees offered food for inspiration.

"Gather away," she replied, and they both scurried to the task, gathering dozens of the smooth, round hazelnuts.

They retrieved their horses and set off across the river. The swift waters narrowed at the twist, barely passable on horseback. Even with the river flowing at its lowest—these days between summer and winter—their horses walked chest deep in the silver liquid. Several large fish jumped out of the water, their pinkish-red bodies shining in the sunlight.

"What I wouldn't give for a salmon. What d'ya think Gobann meant? What would happen if we ate one?" Wynn asked.

"I don't know really, but these fish live and breathe in the magic waters. One swig of it gives us a boost; can you imagine being steeped in it as they are? They're probably as old as the river itself. To kill and eat something that special seems as wrong as . . . eating a unicorn or something."

Wynn grimaced. "There goes my appetite."

They reached the opposite shore and headed south along the riverbank edging the dense woods.

"Over there, that's where we first came upon the river." Wynn pointed to the opposite riverbank. "I think we should start heading east."

Lia eyed the gloomy forest as she followed him. They maneuvered the horses through the bracken, undergrowth, and roots, making unhurried but steady progress. The farther they distanced themselves from the life-giving river, the bleaker the woods became.

Lia had closed off her senses to the wood, not wanting to become overwhelmed, but the forest called to her anyway. She peered at the tall trees, some the palest gray, others dark as pitch, and all covered with eerie black diamonds pitted along their bark.

"Is that noise from the trees?" Wynn's face aimed skyward. The whisper of countless leaves shivered from the limbs.

"Uh-huh, these are the *Eadhas*, aspen trees." Lia recalled Grandma Myrna's summons from deep in the mountain stream, "Find me at the headless *Eadha* . . ."

She hesitated before reaching out to them, searching her memory for their lore. Their inner bark and roots were useful on cuts and wounds, and skillful hands could craft fever tonics. A shiver

195

crossed her shoulders as she remembered a verse from the *Grimoire:*

— *Quaking tree with leaves a flutter,*
Your whispers I do hear;
Taunted by doom, endless tests of courage,
And battles waged against fear.

Lia related to their fear. The edge of *Straif* territory filled her with plenty of it.

Very slowly, she reached out her mind to them. She immediately heard their calls, their warnings of danger and torment, and she felt them tremble in fright. Sorrow pressed on her heart as their whispers turned to sobs. They cried of their plight as prisoners, cried about their wretched fate, how they never knew when their time would come, never knew when their torture would begin, the pain, suffering, despair . . .

Enough! Lia commanded, and she released from the trees before they revealed any more of their woes.

"What is it?" Wynn asked. "You look like you're going to be sick."

"The trees are tormented." She breathed deeply. "Something very dark and dismal haunts the *Eadhas.*"

His brow creased and his jaw set hard, and he grasped the hilt of his sword. They trudged on for hours through the dreary woods. Lia grew hypnotized by the steady gait of her horse. The dense forest and mist blocked out the sky, hiding the sun's passage, but she guessed by her incessant yawns that the day waned toward its end.

"Let's find a place to camp," she said.

Wynn nodded beneath the hood of his cloak.

They found the largest clearing they could, which barely contained them, and they scraped through mounds of pungent, mildewed leaves to create a smoother surface.

Lia's hands turned red and numb with cold as they fished under arms of entwining ivy for remnants of firewood. After persistent scavenging, they claimed a decent supply of dry tinder, and she retrieved her kettle while Wynn struck the fire. The flames cut through the dreadful mist, but the heat barely took the chill from their shivering bodies.

Wynn held his mug close. "Dare I ask what I'm drinking?"

"My two sleepy friends—maythens and melissa."

They drank their tea and ate roasted hazelnuts in silence, and then huddled close to draw added warmth from each other. Lia reached up to pull her hair across her chin, but her hand came back empty and cold. She squeezed her eyes shut and fell asleep amid the tremulous whispers of the trees.

Chilling mist drapes across her sight and she stumbles to find her way. Horrid, relentless fog! Sinister laughter pierces her ears, that same mirthless cackle she's heard over and over before. Wretched Straif! But wait. Can it be? Then a strange, haunting voice echoes through the haze, "Ahhh, child of enchanted blood, 'tis your fate that beckons you to me. Daughter mage, kin to the doomed, your time draws you near."

Stump

U p already?" Wynn grogged, peeling one eye open. "What is it, what's wrong?"

"Another dreadful fate-dream, but this time it, or rather he, spoke to me."

"Who, the *Straif?*" Wynn persisted, rubbing his eyes.

Lia shuddered. "I had thought it was—always with that horrid laughter—but now that I know the voice of trees, I realize it's something else. Something worse."

Wynn untangled himself from his bedding, grabbed his water skin, and handed it to her. "Here. You look queasy."

"Thanks." She took a drink and shrugged. Whatever haunted her dreams would not stop them from pressing forward. "Best get moving."

They packed up their things under the pre-dawn sky like two

dragons puffing smoke into the icy air. With an apple between her teeth, Lia mounted Merrie. The charmed fruit brought renewed vigor to her senses, helping to purge some of the gloom from her mind.

The horses moved slowly through the mist while Lia's mind took flight. She thought about the *Grimoire*, about her dreams, her connection with trees, and about the visions that her quartz had bestowed. All gifts, tools to help her. The last quartz vision had shown her grandmother's birth and her great-grandmother's death. It was a bittersweet day to mark the beginning of Grandma's magic.

With her legs held firm against Merrie, Lia yanked forth her pack, dove both hands into it, and began combining herbs. She drew from her memory what the old widow used. Ailm *needles, sage, candlewick, dew of the sea, muggons, and, yes of course, fennel, dead-nettles, and elf leaf.* She placed the blend in a pouch dangling from her wrap belt, the same concoction thrown over the grave of Grandma's mother.

Now, to recall that strange chant the widow rattled off. Lia searched her mind and the voice of the crone resounded in her head.

"*Expello captivus phasma,*" Lia murmured. The words rolled from her mouth as if she tasted their strange, yet familiar sound. The second part of the chant echoed forth and she spun out the words like silk: "*Arcesso imperium caelestis.*"

She nodded in satisfaction against the frigid mist, continuing to run the incantation over in her mind. It was old magic and powerful enough to reach the dead.

So, why hadn't the valuable chant been included among the passages in the

Grimoire?

She was certain the old women had passed their knowledge onto Grandma Myrna. Maybe Grandma thought it best to guard those secrets, believing the words too potent to scrawl on parchment. Or perhaps they were a part of her writings, but the pages were hidden like the scroll found in Granda's cane.

Lia had so much to share, so many questions to ask Granda. His familiar image pressed on her mind, his woolly beard and sapphire eyes, his steady voice and manner. She thought of him working in his gardens, carefully tending to the herbs, and she choked back a rush of tears.

A sennight had passed—seven long days—since they left Granda and Kelven behind. *So much time.* She refused to think the worst; Da and Granda held strong, Ebrill's herbs fought the poison, and she and Wynn would be home soon, away from this place with the elixir in hand.

Her mind continued to wrestle her worries, as she and Wynn forged through the thickening mists, unable to tell the time of day, and barely able to see past one another. When the haze finally lifted, Lia noticed the change.

The *Eadha* trees stood pitch-dark, as if charred, and she opened her senses enough to feel their trembling life forces ebb into nothingness. The entire forest had grown black as death, including the soil, suffused by the ghostly mist that hung like a pall. Birdsongs and the hurried scuttles of animals ceased, and Nolan and Merrie became jumpy in the stillness.

"Mighty grim landscape," Wynn grumbled. "Looks like heavier mist ahead, too. If it persists, we won't be able to tell where the woodland mists end and the wall of Brume begins."

A cold chill crept up Lia's spine. Brume's eastern border had to be near, along with its torrent of shades. She'd hear them, see them, and this time she didn't hold Grandma's amber—

A great rustling stirred below. Merrie reared up and Lia held tight to avoid falling backward. "Whoa!" she shouted, the leather reins slicing into her palms.

The frantic mare came down stomping as numerous roots coiled up like black serpents before them.

The Straif*!*

A great beam of light pierced through the haze, and Wynn swung his glowing sword through the tangled mass. The *Straif's* arms slithered back in retreat, vanishing underground as quickly as they came.

Lia scoured the ground, catching sight of a segment that Wynn had cut free. She slid from Merrie and dodged to grab it.

"Lee, no!" Wynn leapt down to her side.

"It's a piece." She scooped up the *Straif's* finger, bending it gently, and a long thorn flipped upward. *Tricky.* The telltale spikes were held flat until needed, perhaps for better travel, or perhaps to better entangle a victim until ready to inject its poison.

She held it in her hand, raw from the reins, and the black

misshapen member exuded the frailest bit of life. Within the few seconds before it faded away, Lia felt a wisp of its essence, and her heart skipped.

"It's a prisoner, Wynn. The *Straif* tree's a tool, controlled by another."

"But what about that spiel you gave about the baneful *Straif* with wicked thorns that cut like a knife, and so on?" Wynn eyed her fixedly. "You know, it doesn't matter. It doesn't matter who or what's in charge because we have the piece, don't you see? We've got what we came for to make the elixir. We can head south now, away from the *Straif* and this incessant mist before we make our way through Brume's fog."

He was right. She held the needed ingredient in the palm of her hand and it had come surprisingly easy. *Too easy*, she worried.

"We can't turn back yet. We still have to find the headless *Eadha* where the black waters roil. Grandma is waiting."

"Waiting for what?" Wynn shook his head. "Grandma's gone from this world, Lee. Your da, Granda, and all the others are still here fighting to stay *alive*."

"Yes, I know," she murmured. "And I wish for nothing else than to get home and help them. But we have to go on. I can't explain it, Wynn, but I know if we don't find Grandma first, it will all be for nothing."

"So this is it," he said, eyes as cold as the mists. "All is lost unless we find a ghost in this forsaken wood."

Lia swallowed hard and nodded.

He ran a rough hand through his blond shag. "All right, Lee. You understand this shadow land better than I. Lead the way."

Lia tucked away the *Straif* segment, gripped her loaded crossbow in front of her, and cantered Merrie ahead. They traveled onward, stopping only to give the horses a drink from the water skins. The view dragged on like an infinite world of murk, and Lia figured it had to be well past midday. She wondered if they'd lost all sense of direction and by some cruel trick travelled in circles. But when the forest shifted into a new realm of nightmares, she knew they'd finally arrived.

Miserable stumps replaced hundreds of once tormented *Eadha* trees. Now, only headless *Eadhas* filled the landscape. Sorrow washed through Lia, the kind of deep and woeful sadness that drowns all hope. Her mind and body shuddered in her struggle against the overwhelming misery. Then she spotted it—a massive black stump with clouds of steam pouring forth.

She slowly approached, scanning the ground, watching for any sign of movement. Wynn matched her stride, his sword and shield beacons of defense. Everything but the roiling steam appeared barren. The grove was like a silent grave. They approached the stump and slipped off their horses.

Lia stepped to the base of the headless *Eadha*, catching the slightest whiff of the fetid odor. "It's some sort of cauldron."

She drew her cloak over her mouth and peered closer into the boiling abyss, then whirled around at Wynn's shout, "The ground, Lee, it's moving!"

The black roots of the *Straif* swirled beneath Wynn's feet. Merrie and Nolan reared and backed away, but numerous thick arms shot up and grabbed the horses' legs. Within seconds, the roots pulled both horses to the ground and bound them there.

Wynn swung his sword wildly, slicing through the countless arms reaching up around him. His shield glared at the *Straif*, reflecting the pythonic roots aiming to strike.

Lia stood against the base of the *Eadha*, her crossbow useless against the menacing *Straif*. Wynn's blade sliced the *Straif*'s arms to pieces; black shoots flung into perished bits. But no matter how many roots his blade cut through, endless more reached up to take their place.

Lia leapt toward the trapped horses, but with her first step, woody arms shot up before her. The *Straif* twisted into a tall open-topped cage, walling her and the *Eadha* stump inside.

"Nooo!" She tugged madly at the fibrous roots. Frantic, she grabbed her knife and sawed at one of them. Fleeting satisfaction filled her as she severed her way through, but then more shoots drew up from the soil, strengthening the cage once again.

Wynn fought on. His battle cries had turned hoarse, but his movements held swift and sure. The gnashing barbs carved trails of blood across his face and hands. He stood knee deep in severed arms of the *Straif*, a black sea of death that grew by the second.

Merrie and Nolan lay pinned, their muzzles pressed and frothing against the menacing ropes.

"Please! Let them go!" Lia yanked at her immovable prison, but stopped at the sudden tingling in her hands.

The sensation emanated from the *Straif's* limbs, its energy like tiny needles of heat running under her skin. Lia struggled to quiet her panic and dared to connect with the tree. She sensed the *Straif's* haggard and bitter nature, its cold determination to obey the bidding of some unseen master.

She leaned her head against the *Straif's* arms and probed deeper, peeling through the layers of apathy, delving beneath the scars of slavery, to the tree's true essence. Then a force pulled Lia's focus to the east.

Her mind flew through the mists like an arrow hitting its target. There among the *Eadha* stumps, grew a dark twisted shrub tree with yellowing leaves and purple-black sloe berries. The *Straif* tree was motionless while its roots battled Wynn's blade. Just like its strangled victims, the tree suffered from shackles imposed by a ruthless captor. Who the captor was though, Lia couldn't tell.

"Hear me, wild *Straif.* Stop your attack. Use your strength to break free from your captor—"

Lia's connection with the tree splintered and she choked for air. The *Eadha* stump boiled fiercer, the steaming miasma setting off waves of nausea within her belly. Its waters smelled of death, rotten and vile, like the stench from a thousand corpses. She fell to the

205

ground and sucked in fresher air, but it did nothing to diminish her nausea.

Her eyes watered and she retched, the sweet apples and hazelnuts now bitter on her tongue. She gritted her teeth and willed her body to still. Then, like ice running down her spine, a familiar voice oozed forth. "Ahhh, here you finally are."

Lia lifted her head and peered into the clouds of steam. "Who . . . what are you?"

She stood, pulled her cloak over her mouth, and breathed through its thick cloth. "Why don't you show yourself instead of hiding behind some wretched tree?" She swooned and coughed under the fumes, commanding her insides not to spew again.

"Brave girl. Good. Your fire will serve me well." An enormous black shroud loomed over the open top of her cage.

"Shade!" Lia's eyes froze in terror.

This shade eclipsed the tattered forms of the Scalachs. Never had she seen this hue of blackness, as if its body had sucked every ray of light, every tiny glimmer into its enormous form. She strained to find the borders of its body, barely making out where the edges blackness met the fog's gray.

The faceless anomaly pressed down, undulating over her like an ocean of pitch. "I am Draugryd, master to the Scalach legions."

Lia's knees nearly buckled and her voice stuck in her throat. A gust of wind shot forth as numerous smaller shrouds plunged through the mist like ink splatters. Their awful moans followed, filling her mind with, "Lia, Lia . . . ." Her emptied stomach revolted, and she fell to the ground, clawing at the soil as her gut heaved.

Wynn roared his fury at the winds beating against him. He swung his blade high in the air, and though he had no sight for the dead, Lia watched him hack through numerous Scalach shades. With every sword thrust, their black shredded bodies disintegrated into dust, extinguishing their foul gusting breath forever. Laguz had been right, the sword cut through anything, even creatures roaming from the Underworld.

Lia's voice freed. "You're destroying them, Wynn—the shades above you—you're tearing them apart!"

Wynn fought wildly, his strength and stamina enduring, his weaponry unmatched. His yellow hair shone under the light of his sword like a crown of gold. *A true king's heir*, she thought.

"He fights well, for a boy," Draugryd mocked, his voice grating against Lia's mind. "He's quite amusing to watch. But even with that glamour-blade, he is one against untold many. It's only a matter of time before he falls."

Lia seethed at his cruelty. "Coward! Call off the *Straif*, call off your wretched army, and stand alone."

A chilling stillness followed—the thrashing *Straif's* arms fell in a heap, the Scalach shades flew away, and the air hushed. All at once, the mists darkened and the winds roused into a howling rage.

Fierce gales slammed Lia like a rag doll against her cage bars. She barely caught her breath before the gusts tossed her into a somersault and she landed with a thunk at the base of the stump. She curled her body tight against the *Eadha*, grasping at the shredded remains of her ma's cloak. Wynn had no such shelter, and through blurred eyes, Lia saw him fight against Draugyrd's storm.

The winds ripped his enchanted shield from his arm. The blaze of metal flung high and away as if the shining lindwyrm dragon on it took flight. He took countless gusts from all sides, his cloak whipping around him in tatters. His face and arms, his sun-yellow hair, all ran scarlet in the frenzied winds beating against flesh and bone. And though his mouth gaped open, his scream evaporated into silence.

In one final effort, Wynn swung his sword, and then collapsed to the ground.

"No!" Lia's scream turned to sobs. "Oh, please wake up, Wynn. I'm sorry. I shouldn't have provoked Draugyrd. Please, don't die!"

Fresh *Straif* roots coiled around his arms and legs. Only the glowing blade beside him remained untouched by the *Straif*. The winds died in victory and the dark waters of the *Eadha* stump calmed.

Lia unfolded her trembling body and rose from the ground, tears streaming down her face. Draugyrd hovered somewhere in the fog above, laughing. *Wretched demon!* Then her eyes fell to the lingering vapors of steam taking form before her. And her breath seized in her throat.

She was now face to face with Grandma Myrna.

Taproot

*L*ia clenched the stump and barely uttered, "Grandma." The copper-haired woman floated like silks on the clouds of steam with her face creased in misery.

Their eyes met, green-to-green, and Grandma Myrna's voice rang urgent."He craves yer soul, child, enchanted blood touched by the *Nion*—"

"Silence!" Draugyrd's command echoed through Lia's mind, ripping away Grandma's voice. His mass came down like a suffocating mantle.

Grandma Myrna floated in silence, though her eyes screamed in terror. Lia aimed her face up into the inky abyss of Draugyrd, willing her legs to stand firm. "Vile wraith! Why do you bind her?"

"Is it so hard to understand?" he said. "I desire what all great rulers do: no less than total dominion. And your elder has summoned the key—you."

He paused, letting Lia grapple with the notion, and then continued, "I've used your kinswoman's essence to charm the *Straif,* dominate these *Eadhas,* even be-spell a *Ruis* tree, all passable efforts to touch the living. But that is the limit to her powers. You, on the other hand, shall serve in carrying out my ultimate conquest. With your magic, I shall force the trees across the lands under my control, and through them, each and every earthly soul will become bound to me."

Each and every soul?

Lia's body shook. A vivid picture of his plan flashed inside her head. He would use her inborn gifts, her wisdom of nature, and her connection with the trees to form a massive root system from the *Eadhas* in his dismal grove. The monstrosity would thrust forth through the fog, snake underground, and infect every other root in its path. Each leaf, nut, and fruit across the lands would carry his darkness. Earth's vital bounty would bring doom to all.

Draugyrd snickered as the revelation of his plan sank into Lia's mind. "Yes, you see it now; the living will feast upon the poisoned fare. Their flesh will die and their souls will become mine. I shall achieve what none from the Underworld has—total domination over the minions of this world."

Lia shook her head in horror. Draugyrd planned to annihilate every human, every dwarf, and every other race existing in the world.

Then he would shackle their spirits as he had Grandma's.

From her acid-scorched throat, she pushed out the words, "Never, I'll never—"

A gust of wind punched her and knocked her against the stump.

"You *will* obey," Draugyrd said. "There is no fighting me. It is time to join both of your elders."

Both my elders?

Lia's insides turned to ice. Grandma's spirit faded back into the steam, and another image emerged, barely visible. The elder man reached a ghostly hand toward Lia, his winter-white hair and sapphire eyes dissipating on the vapors.

"Nooo!" Lia cried, shaking her head in anguish. *It cannot be . . .* She slid to the ground and her body racked with sobs. "You killed him . . . you killed Granda."

The master shade's laughter drummed against Lia's skull while sorrow strangled her heart. She'd failed Granda. Ebrill's herbs had failed him, too. And now her beloved granda suffered in Draugryd's liquid prison. The shade-demon had taken both her grandparents, and she and Wynn were next.

What of Da? Is his soul suffering in wretched torment with all the others?

"It is over for your kind," Draugyrd sneered, and then his voice turned blithe. "But I am not an ungracious master; I reward those who obey. All you must do is drink. Drink of my waters and your death shall be painless. Disobey me, and die slowly—days, weeks of tortured agony—while I tear your soul piece by piece from your rotting body."

"Vile thief!" Lia choked on her sobs. "Their souls, the *Straif*, the fog, none were ever yours to command."

"You defend the *Straif*, a hag tree that binds your people and poisons them, the very bane killing your companions as we speak?"

Her eyes darted to Wynn's cocooned body. Stifled moans emanated through his thorny shackles. Lying near him, the horses pressed against tangled cages, their eyes bulging and foam escaping from their mouths. Her companions suffered, but Draugyrd spared them from death.

Spared them until they no longer served as leverage.

Draugyrd would use their lives and any other clever way to gain Lia's cooperation. As with any crucial spell, her death required care. Her soul would bind unharmed through the ritual of his roiling brew. Without it, he risked damaging her full magic and his means for total dominion.

The winds died, the roots calmed, and the *Eadha* cauldron stilled. In the quiet of his victory, Draugyrd whispered, "We are not so different, you and I, for you seek the very thing I promise."

Lia shook her head, blinking tear-blurred eyes. "I seek nothing but your ruin!"

He laughed low and deep. "Think of the power. You shall spread your magic across the lands and bring those that would shun you to their knees. You will purge the ignorance befouling the world; your magic will cleanse the lands. You, and you alone, can give the world a chance to start anew."

Draugyrd's words fell on Lia like snowflakes, soft and pristine despite their chill. She wasn't be-spelled as with the *Nion* guardian, but something about Draugyrd's voice swathed her mind in satin and numbed the rawness of her grief.

Purge the ignorance? Cleanse the lands?

Nothing would please her more than to see the royals of the lands fall. They had poisoned their people against nature and magic, and all the world suffered for it.

A cool breeze brushed across Lia's face, and Draugyrd murmured in her mind, "You can give the greatest gift ever given— nature back to itself. Give Nemetona back to its namesake, back to its sacred groves."

The world, the groves, could heal, renew . . . It seemed so clear, so easy, so . . . right. But something tugged at Lia's core. The sensation gave her pause, and she forced her thoughts deeper into Draugyrd's silken words.

Darkness flooded her mind then, followed by jaws snapping, chains dragging, screams, sobs, silence . . . *No!* The smell of burning flesh surrounded her and the taste of blood filled her mouth. *This is the fate he plans for us all. I have to find a way to stop this . . . distract him . . . The quartz!*

She clawed at her tunic, grasping in desperation for what was no longer there.

"Looking for this?" Draugyrd stirred a cloud of mist around the pouch resting several feet from her cage. "Tsk, tsk. Seems during your tumble those winds must've swept it right from you."

Lia's mouth gaped and she shook in horror. He had ripped away her talisman. Now sword, shield, and stone, all three weapons of hope, lay useless on the ground.

"Didn't think I'd miss that, did you? I knew you held it the minute you first entered my fog. Why do you think my horde harassed you so? Gave us all a start, like tiny daggers pricking away, and even now, like a pesky sting . . . but no matter. Away from your touch, it holds little power. Just like the towers enchanting the fog: ignored, untouched, forgetting their purpose."

The master shade draped his curtain around Lia's prison, enveloping her in his darkness. His body oozed like tar around the arms of her cage, and he sent tentacles to brush against her. The feel of him on her skin was nothing like she imagined. His substance was more akin to mists than tar, though unlike mist, his touch burned across her flesh.

Hoarse gasps slid from her lips and she clutched at the stump. *No . . . please . . .* Shoots slithered up her legs, and the *Straif's* arms coiled around her. Her mind screamed in revolt, her body twisted, and the ancient tree cried out to her.

Lia froze in her struggle and connected with the *Straif.* The tree revealed an image of itself, as if displaying a painting from long ago. In it, half of the tree hid within the shadows, and the other half blazed bright. Lia held onto the image, and like the dawn, the tree's stark wisdom emerged:

> *Darkness exists so that light may shine;*
> *By its very nature, darkness gives power to light.*

Lia wondered how powerful the light was that Draugyrd gave rise to.

She drew strength from the crone tree and her fear of the master shade began to lessen. Draugyrd's anger stirred within her newfound calm. The *Straif* had eluded his control for a moment, but fell to his command once more. The roots squeezed tighter and yanked Lia toward the fetid waters.

"Drink!" Draugyrd's voice boomed inside her head.

Several thorns turned upward, penetrating deep into her legs. She bit back the pain and begged the *Straif* to stop, to break free as she had done a moment ago, but the slave-tree remained strangled by the shade's power.

Sweat beaded across Lia's brow and her stomach tightened as the pungent waters sizzled. Wispy figures swam through the cauldron, their lithe bodies twisting aimlessly.

So many, she thought, *so many tormented souls trapped in his foul brew.*

"Now!" Draugyrd's screech tore through Lia's mind. His Scalach army rallied close, chanting her name in unison.

She stumbled forward and her head grew fuzzy, the *Straif's* poison surging through her veins. Her eyelids drooped and her jaw went slack. All she wanted was to curl on the ground and sleep.

"That's it, heed my wishes and you'll have your rest."

Rest, yes. Get this over with and then I can close my eyes.

Her head rolled forward, her silver crown bowed over the waters, and she reached her arm toward the pool of souls. *Like fish,* she thought dreamily, and the dwarf scout's words drifted in her mind, "Best not t'fish from the Seren River. Enchanted waters poured straight from the heart of Brume. Life's special, sacred within 'em."

Sacred life . . . heart of Brume . . . Brume's blood!

Lia grasped the water skin hanging from her belt. Like a great vessel carrying magic from the mountains, the Seren River provided Brume's lifeblood. The *Nion* guardian had told her to use a bit of Brume's blood on the *Straif;* it was also a part of the elixir. The sacred waters nurtured and healed life, while Draugyrd took it away. The clever master had missed the one thing Lia held that countered his very essence.

With her heart racing, she drew up the skin, released the stopper, and dumped the silver water into the cauldron. Hissing steam poured forth, the rotten odor muted, and Draugyrd and his army dashed skyward.

The mass of darkness swirled above the plumes of steam, and a cacophony of shrieks tore across the forest. With its master distracted, the *Straif* tree relaxed its grip, and Lia reached a trembling hand down to her crossbow. She emptied a remaining stream of enchanted water onto the bolt's tip, forced her shaky hands to still, and released. The bolt flew through the bars of her cage, through the mists, and pierced the base of the *Straif.*

Lia shuddered. Her sense of the haggard tree grew as Brume's silver blood ran life through it. The magic waters ran through root, trunk, and limb, freeing the *Straif* from the binding spell. Lia thought sure the crone tree snorted, like an old woman huffing as she tossed aside a corset. In one great shake, the thorny *Straif* shed its mutated roots like the skins of a thousand snakes. With its baneful arms discarded, its true roots stretched in relief.

Rockberg, the Bryns, and all the other villages of Nemetona were now safe from the venomous scourge. But Lia could only wonder at the full measure of destruction wreaked by the *Straif.* Or rather, by Draugyrd.

The spiny *Straif* breathed with renewed vigor, though its essence remained sour, much like the sloes that dangled amongst its razor-sharp thorns. Lia's connection faded from the *Straif*, the tree free to soak in the misty air and wish for a long winter.

Wynn groaned and stuggled through the limp branches, and Lia made her way over her wilting cage to his side. Though her strength waned thin, she helped him to a stand. The horses snorted in their efforts to find footing, the tangle of dead limbs falling from their backs. Lia stumbled toward Merrie and grabbed hold of her saddlebag, withdrawing another water skin. "Seren water . . . we all must drink."

The enchanted water would buy them some time. Brume's lifeblood would slow the *Straif's* venom, but for how long, Lia didn't know. Wynn suffered the worst of it. The waters were unable to heal his poisoned gashes, but it staunched the rivers of scarlet pouring from his wounds.

"Lee," Wynn said, looking upward.

Lia whirled around and nearly lost her balance at the sight. The steam was gone, and now a fountain of silver spouted from the headless *Eadha*. Though Wynn spotted the water, he couldn't see the horde of pale and wailing ghosts shooting from it.

The torent of silver poured forth, but a greater mass of ink-black pressed down. Draugyrd hung there, while the Scalach shades whipped against the frail spirits, surrounding and herding them like frightened sheep. The souls flew from one prison into the grasp of another.

Lia grasped the pouch dangling from her belt. Into her palm, she emptied the herbal blend remembered from her vision of the old widows. She threw the herbs high and called out the widow's chant, *"Expello captivus phasma, arcesso imperium caelestis."*

The widow's words poured from her lips, and spirits began to escape. The shades screamed in rage, a frenzy of high-pitched shrills, as their prisoners fled. On and on Lia called out the chant, louder, faster, until the great multitude of souls flew free.

Grandma's voice rang beside her then. "Be gone captive spirits, by the power of celestial light." Grandma Myrna flitted overhead, a glowing specter. "Ye've done it, child, wielded the invocation with an untainted heart. Ye've released them to the Summerlands, Granda

Luis too. He's at peace and prouder than ever of ye both. But we've little time before the master rallies his power and comes for ye again. The stone, child; retrieve yer stone."

Lia choked back a river of tears and shot toward the *Eadha* stump, now barren and cold. She grasped her pouch nestled near the crumpled roots of her cage and released the crystal into her palm. Its fiery heat raged forth and she focused her mind, delving deep within the ancient quartz. She allowed it to draw from her energy, as she called out a single command, "Help us!"

A blinding light beamed outward, purging the surrounding mists. The faceless bodies of shades twisted wildly beyond its fringes, and Grandma shouted, "Hold onto its power, and once I'm inside, ye must race like the wind."

Inside?

Lia held on to the crystal's force, its span of burning light enclosing her within it. Grandma's spirit hovered and she reached wispy arms out to Lia's stone.

"You must race to the great *Idho!*" Grandma Myrna cried before her soul poured like a stream of water into the quartz. The burning light pulled inward, sealing the elder inside the crystal sanctuary.

Lia's jaw dropped. Not only had Grandma anchored herself within the magic quartz, she had stayed behind instead of flying with the others to paradise. Wynn was right about the elixir. She was the maiden and Grandma was the blood-kin crone. And the final part of the cure.

Lia tucked her stone away and mounted Merrie. Wynn stared at her from atop Nolan, waiting, and she called out, "To the south!"

They charged forth, the silver waters giving their horses strength. Wynn rode beside her with his sword and shield in his grip. His bond to the weapons had become like hers with the crystal. They were his talismans, their magic wielded by the essence of their rightful holder.

They fled toward the *Idho*—the tree with the grand hollow from her dream two nights before. It grew at the southeastern tip of the Seren River just beyond the mists. Lia knew it waited for them, like a towering giant offering its body as a haven.

The bleak forest whipped by and Lia dared to think of home, dared to hope that her da lived, and that she still had time to heal him. She pictured him strong and laughing, sanding down a table or hutch chest. She loved the smell of his workshop, the fresh wood shavings, lemon infused oils, and sweet blocks of beeswax. He'd ask, "What d'ya think, Lia? Good enough for someone's house or should we just put it out on the back porch?" Her reply was always the same, "Only the finest house will do." His whole face would smile with pride.

Tears stung her eyes and her face froze in the chilled air. They maneuvered through the last of the *Eadha* stumps and the forest rose tall once again, the trees green with life. Her heart pounded with anticipation. They were almost free. But as they passed the first of the pale trees, an onslaught of winds beat against them.

Terror washed through Lia. "Shades!"

"We have to find cover." Wynn's battered face ran with fresh blood.

The Idho. *We have to get to the* Idho. Through the howling winds, Lia reached out her mind, straining to feel the tree's essence. "Wynn, get to the yew tree on the riverbank, less than half a league!"

She buried her face within Merrie's tangled mane. Her horse pressed against the driving storm. The drum of the *Idho's* call grew louder, the ancient tree beckoning her. The winds raged, the mists darkened, and she lost sight of Wynn through the blinding gales. Not even his glowing blade answered her frantic cries. The pull of the *Idho* held her path straight, but her cousin had no such anchor. She had to find him before he vanished forever.

She drew out her pouch. Heat penetrated the leather from the quartz within, the promise of magic answering her. But before she could release the stone, a hard gust punched her, knocking her face first to the ground.

Hollow

*L*ia landed in a flash of stars. She swam through the murk of unconsciousness, struggling for air. With a great heave she awoke, but nearly fainted again from the racking pain. Jagged stones and dead *Eadha* branches cut into her flesh. Like cruel hands, the winds ripped bloodied shreds from her ma's cloak.

"Wake, child! He's coming."

Lia lifted her battered head from the ground and squinted at Grandma.

"Hurry!" Grandma Myrna flickered in and out of view.

Lia's head throbbed and blood ran down her chin, the taste of salt and copper on her tongue. She grabbed her pouch, and this time released the fiery quartz. She barely uttered, "Protect us."

Her insides tugged from the draw of power. Then a brilliant light shot from the stone, forcing back the Scalach's winds. Lia rose on shaking legs and grasped Merrie's reins for support. Her knees nearly buckled from the shooting pains in her ribs. Merrie nuzzled her, both an offering and plea for comfort.

Grandma Myrna's spirit drew closer. "Quickly, Lia."

"Have to . . . find . . . Wynn." With every step, her energy waned and her body ached in revolt.

Terror etched across Grandma's face.

Lia stumbled through the woods. She kept hold of Merrie's reins and Grandma Myrna followed closely. The wild storm raged beyond their circle of light, its wrath useless against the quartz's power. Wynn had to be near; they had separated only minutes before she fell.

Lia delved her mind into the stone, imploring the magic to expand. Her insides shuddered at the pull of energy. The vast light shot out arms like sunrays. She swiveled her head to each of its beacons and caught a glimpse of something glowing.

"Wynn!" Her call rang loud within the protective sphere. She maneuvered toward him, guided by the glow of his weapons. Nolan's head bowed against the driving winds, his muzzle nudging Wynn's crumpled body.

Lia fell on her knees beside him. The crystal's light encircled them all in safety. She gently rolled her cousin over and gasped. Blood poured from his broken nose, and gashes lined his cheeks and forehead.

She grabbed her water skin, propped his head, and poured a

silver stream into his mouth. She folded a tattered edge of her cloak and dabbed his face with the enchanted liquid, but he did not wake. Her own strength withered, and she hurried and drank some of the water. The quartz responded to her replenished energy. Its light grew brighter, and within its embrace, Wynn's weapons radiated like fire. Even the lindwyrm dragon on his shield sparkled. She continued to wash Wynn's wounds and pour little streams into his mouth.

"He's upon us!" Grandma Myrna screeched.

Lia peered at the edges of her crystal's light. Draugyrd's mass came down and enshrouded their bubble-like haven. Her breath stuck in her throat, but she held to her stone's magic.

Stay strong, keep the light, push him away!

The *Idho's* drum beat its promise of freedom, but Lia's hope fell with each passing moment that Wynn lay motionless on the ground. Her body wavered, the stone using up more and more of her energy. It took every bit of her concentration to maintain the sphere of light.

Then the master shade's words poured forth like venom, "Foolish girl, you cannot escape. Your fate is with me."

"Never!" she shouted. "I choose my fate."

"Ah, the ignorance of youth." Draugyrd's voice cut into her mind like daggers. "No, child, your elder kinswoman bound your destiny to me a long time ago."

"More lies," she spat. "Nothing but trickery."

She shifted her eyes on Grandma. Grandma Myrna's ghost froze like chiseled stone. Lia peered at her, imploring her to argue

Draugyrd's words, but she remained silent.

"No, little pawn, no more faery tales," Draugyrd continued. "Your clever elder used your mother's womb well, a living cauldron for her potions. There she brewed into your tiny body a desire to work magic, a longing for Brume, and imposed a fate upon you to serve her selfish needs."

Lia tried to shut off his voice, but it strangled her mind and forced her to listen. "She made sure you'd follow in her ways. She left you all the right tools, even an elder kinsman to teach you, spellbound by her charms. All because she sold her soul for years of passage into Brume, and then didn't want to pay her end. You became her only hope for escape. When you came to Brume, as she knew you eventually would, she summoned you from the streams. You see, poor girl, all this time, you've been bound to a fate forced upon you by a cowardly hag whose soul dims under the brilliance of your own."

"No, that's not the way. Grandma wouldn't use Ma . . . Granda . . . me . . ." Lia faltered, her world tilting upside down. Grandma Myrna hovered near Lia in wretched silence. Everything Lia believed and revered about her grandmother began to drown in a flood of doubt.

Did Grandma sell her soul, her daughter's womb, and the souls of her grandchildren to gain passage to Brume?

All that Lia upheld, everything she'd strived to immolate, fell like sand through her fingers. Was she kin to lies and deceit, an outcast

225

whose elder had joined forces with the very thing trying to destroy her?

Nothing made sense. The world spun like a spindle pulling away every strand of reason from Lia. Tears spilled down her face, for herself, for Granda, for Ma and Da, and everyone suffering at the hands of her grandmother's magic.

Draugyrd's haughty snicker filled the air. "The ring of truth resounds clear and your elder knows it. So now, it is truly over. No more games; you are no longer her little pawn. Show the courage your kin failed to show and face your destiny."

Lia's distress weakened her energy. The crystal's light shrunk, barely encompassing them. She gazed at Grandma, and though her kinswoman remained mute, her eyes softened to warm pools. Warmth streamed into Lia as thoughts of the *Grimoire* filled her mind.

Of course. Her book!

If anything revealed her grandmother's truth, it was the beloved *Grimoire*. Lia recalled the healing recipes, the wondrous legends, riddles, and sketches, every word and brush stroke showing her love of nature. Understanding radiated within Lia.

Grandma Myrna placed both hands over her heart, a family gesture Lia knew well. *Yes, I love you too*, Lia gestured back, her heart freed from uncertainty.

Lia's memory unraveled the truth. Grandma Myrna had brewed up special potions for Ma, but not the way Draugyrd described. She tended to her daughter's body with loving care, feeding her herbs and tonics to assure a strong pregnancy and healthy babe. Ma claimed that without Grandma's help, she'd have surely been childless. "I was born with a fussy womb," she often said. "Bittersweet is the taste of Brume. It stole my ma away, but the bounty she gathered there helped me give birth to you."

The knowledge Grandma gained from her widow-mothers, her birth bond with the fog, and her strange inborn gifts had instilled within her a clear life's mission: keep the old ways alive, and bring magic and healing to those suffering under a destructive rule. No king, no one claiming sovereign rule, had the right to discard nature's gifts. These riches were the rights of every living creature.

Yes, Lia thought. Grandma sacrificed her life to gain access to the treasures of Brume. *And yes*, she left behind the tools for her kin to carry on. But not for selfish need. She did it to ensure that all those she loved and all those they touched would thrive.

Draugyrd was wrong. Grandma had carried out her end of the bargain—wielding the amber, enchanting food and ale for the Scalach shades, leaving a bit of her spirit each time. She knew her soul would end up in the fog—the place of her birth—for eternity. What she never thought possible, was how Draugyrd would use her spirit against everyone and everything she held dear.

The fateful verse rang out in Lia's mind:

> *For the call of magic, I do what I must;*
> *Sacrifice is needed, to do what is just.*
> *The dark master beckons, and his command I do heed;*
> *Anything I will do for flower, root, and seed.*
> *And after my life does perish,*

And the magic fades toward its end,
I know the children will come forth and bring it back again.

Lia glanced at her sleeping cousin and knew they were part of "the children" coming forth to bring magic back to the lands. They would find a way to purge the imposed stupor from the people of Nemetona, strengthen the crystals' enchantment of Brume's fog, and expel Draugyrd and his ruthless horde back to the pits of the Underworld. The lands would thrive once again, but not by the poisons of Draugyrd.

"You are right, Master Shade," Lia said simply. "I must stand and face my destiny."

Draugyrd paused, loosening his grip, and Lia summoned her remaining strength and poured it into the quartz.

The light expanded, shoving the powerful shade back. He bellowed in fury, nearly shaking Lia's skull apart. His forest turned to a dark blur as hurricane winds tore the surrounding trees apart. She pushed aside her grief for the tormented woods and held on to the magic.

Draugyrd raged against the bright sphere, his pitchy mass crashing upon the light in waves. Sweat poured down Lia's face, her body shook, and her head ached. Just when she was near collapse, Wynn rose beside her. He thrust his blade through the border of light and pierced Draugyrd's mass.

Draugyrd, the wild storm, and the surrounding mists flew deep into the confines of Brume's fog, as if sucked there by some unworldly void. All turned quiet and still. Wynn's blade shone clean, as if he'd pierced nothing but mist, but Lia knew the sword's magic had burned through the shade. She'd heard his cries of pain before his voice silenced.

"Gone to lick his wounds," Grandma Myrna said. "He'll be needing a fine measure of tending to, to regain his power. Then only time will tell. But ye've done it, dear ones. Together ye've triumphed."

"That voice . . . a woman." Wynn's eyes shone against his haggard face.

Lia quickly faced him. "You can *hear* Grandma?"

He stumbled and gripped his side. "I heard a few words, like a whisper."

"You're hurt, Wynn." Lia reached out to him, but he put his hand up to stop her.

"I'm all right, just a bit broken inside." He creased his brow. "What? Why the strange look?"

Lia gently traced the sharp pattern painted on his sandy hair. "Running through a misty forest with jagged white streaks in your hair."

His eyes widened. "Don't tell me that dream of yours came true?"

She nodded, dumbstruck.

Wynn blew out his breath and shook his head. "How 'bout we get out of here now?"

Grandma Myrna smiled at them and her spirit slipped back into the quartz, the light drawing in behind her. Lia cupped the crystal in a gentle embrace before she tucked it within her pouch.

Her eyes roved the battered forest, now cleared of mist. The surviving trees reached out to her in gratitude. Though many had been injured or killed, life prevailed. For now, this wood lived free from Draugyrd's grasp.

Wynn nearly passed out again mounting Nolan, and Lia handed him a root. "Chew on this; it should help some of the pain. Not much more we can do now for cracked ribs."

They edged the last of the *Eadhas* and Lia spotted a small gnarled tree in a barren plot. It was the elder, or *Ruis* tree, that Draugyrd used Grandma's magic to be-spell. *For some wretched purpose, to be sure.*

Its crooked limbs reached out to her like arms, the corky wood covered in blood-red leaves and purple-black berries. One of its more grim nicknames, "Tree of Doom," fit quite well after the master shade's touch. Lia felt nothing of the tree's essence, and sensed only emptiness, like a hollow shell of its long forgotten life. Even so, it called to her.

She veered Merrie toward the tree, her heart pounding like a death march.

"Lee, what are you doing?"

"This tree is enchanted, turned baneful like the *Straif* and the *Eadha* cauldron. It must be set free." She slid from Merrie's back and crept to the base of the tree. She ran her fingers over the gray ridges of the *Ruis* wood, sensing how the spell had emptied the tree of its true life force. Then she reached up to the berries dangling above. Tainted fruit, filled with the darkness of Draugyrd. She plucked a small cluster of the fruit and removed them from their lacy stems.

Her chest burned from the heat of her quartz and urgent whispers emanated from Grandma Myrna's spirit.

"It's all right, Grandma. I know what I'm doing."

Lia closed her eyes, pushed beyond her sorrow, and remembered a time when she picked elderberries with Granda. Each autumn they took the ripest of the bitter berries and dried them for eating or mixed them in honey to make syrups. Her mouth watered with the memory of mounds of flat cakes smothered in the liquid delight. The villagers eagerly awaited the fare, buying it up faster than she and Granda Luis could pour it into jars. Ma made sweet jams, muffins, and pies, their market value rivaling her soaps.

Lia clung to the cherished memories, drew up her hand, and promptly dropped the elderberries into her mouth. Their juice tasted surprisingly sweet. A voice came from the depths of the tree then. "Thank you for honoring me." The *Ruis* exhaled with a great tremble before its tortured existence ended.

Lia's head swam, but a sense of peace filled her. Soft light surrounded her and the ground disappeared into nothingness. She lingered in a realm of quiet bliss, as if floating amid the clouds. *So, this is death* . . .

Her eyes flew open to the eerie caw of a rook—an enormous

bird of good omen. The oily black bird flapped its wings and took flight from the *Ruis* tree's altered crown. Lia found her feet and stumbled in awe at the tree's transformation. Like a skeleton, it stood white as bone. Even the leaves and berries hung in alabaster stillness.

A warm hand fell on her shoulder, and she turned. Wynn peered at her. "Lee?"

"It's free now. No more suffering in limbo, no more fruits filled with Draugyrd's poison," she whispered. "I followed its spirit, just for a moment, into the Otherworld."

Wynn's brow drew together. "Are you all right; how do you feel?"

"Oddly relaxed," she said, marveling at her new sensations. Her body still ached, but the harsher pains had vanished. Her eyesight had also intensified. She blinked in wonder. Every hue of color, every essence of plant life, sparkled like gemstones. Her enhanced vision captured auras radiating from every tree in the grove. *A gift from the Otherworld.*

Wynn shook his head. "You were aglow in a strange blue light. It poured from you like a water fountain into the tree. Then all at once, the tree shot out sparks and turned completely white. And so did you."

Lia's eyes fell to her powder-white hands. "Is it . . . just my hands, arms?"

Wynn's silence gave her the answer she dreaded. She reached for his shield and stared at her reflection. Her skin resembled the pale bark of a *Beth* tree, and her eyes had darkened to the hue of an evergreen. She pressed her lips together and released his shield.

So be it, she thought. A glimpse of death, a moment in the Otherworld, had paled her flesh and deepened her sight. Like all her ventures through Brume, she had come away forever changed. And resignation took root within her.

"The blue you saw was a memory, a happy time with Granda cooking up *Ruis* berries." She met Wynn's eyes. "I knew at once how to break the *Ruis* spell, even while Grandma warned me. You were able to hear Grandma's spirit, though you'd never had the gift of ghost speak before. We must've drawn a bit of magic into ourselves when we used our weapons together."

Wynn shrugged. "Nothing would surprise me now."

Lia's heart squeezed and she lifted her eyes to him. "Wynn, Granda's—"

"I already know," he said, his eyes growing moist. "I heard your cry."

Lia's stomach tightened. He'd heard her cries over Granda's death while he lay strangled and helpless in the arms of the *Straif*. She placed her hand on his arm and swallowed down the torrent that threatened to flow.

They rode from the grove and edged the Seren River. On its bank, the *Idho* stretched its arms against a dimming sky. Its reddish bark curved under a crown of needles, and knotholes framed a massive hollow. The opening spanned large enough for the tallest man or beast to enter.

Lia slid off Merrie's back and walked toward the ancient tree. She reached her mind out to it, but her thoughts broke at the sound of howlish barking. She knew this bark. As she stepped toward the hollow, a shag of white spilled forth, and Koun found his way in her arms. His milky fur smelled of dust and home, and she hugged her hound with all her might.

Reseed

K oun," Lia murmured. The hound nuzzled against her and Lia squeezed his great bulk.

Wynn blinked in surprise. "How in ruddy spades?"

"He's come to me again through an *Idho*, like when I first found him in the hollowed tree back in the Bryns."

Lia held his white muzzle between her hands and peered into his eyes—pools of pure violet. "Just like Ebrill's. How did I miss it? You're a fae hound."

"Fae?" Wynn's eyes widened. "Koun's a *faery?*"

"I've heard only one fable about them," Lia said. "Fae hounds cross over from the Otherworld, like fateful messengers between the two realms. Koun must have known about Draugyrd, so he came into our world to help."

"Then why didn't he follow us into Brume, help us fight?"

Lia paused in thought. "Granda wanted him to stay back. He must've known what Koun was, must've known his gifts were better served in the village."

Koun's whine drew their focus, and they followed his eager trot toward the *Idho*. They stepped into the tree's hollow, leading the horses behind them. A subtle orange glow rippled across the inner wood. Wynn held out his sword like a torch to blaze their way.

"Can you feel anything, Lee?" Wynn said. "I mean, can you feel how this tree works? Didn't Gobann say it was like a bridge?"

Lia stilled. She kept one hand on Koun's shaggy backside and placed the other on the *Idho*. She reached out her mind and her thoughts whirled with the tree's memories. Glimpses of its beginnings, thousands of years ago, flashed before her mind's eye.

Ancient groves and meadows spanned the landscape then, and the plantlife was linked together in one breathing network, one grand being. They flourished in abundance, spending endless days nurtured by the rain and wind, the rich soil, and even the cleansing fires of lightning. Working in harmony alongside them lived numerous races of fae.

Koun nudged her, pulling her mind back to the present. "All right, boy, just another moment." She'd have easily spent hours or days reliving the tree's history. She eyed the dark passage at the back of the hollow. *Another portal. This one much different from the Duir.* Tangled roots jutted around its edges like teeth in a gaping maw. She took a breath and aimed her thoughts into its depths.

"It breaks earthly boundaries, Wynn," she said, her mind overwhelmed by the tree's endlessness. "The tunnel splits into numerous paths, each one leading to a different place, many of them realms beyond our own. Some of them converge, some have no end, and I can't be sure which one to take—"

Koun grabbed her wrist into his mouth and pulled.

"Of course," she said, feeling a bit doltish. "We'll follow Koun."

They followed the hound through the orange-red passageway, the horses walking easily through the ample space. Unlike in *Duir's Run*, the ceiling raised high above Wynn's head, though he still slouched from the pain in his ribs. They passed numerous openings, and whispers tickled Lia's ears. She shivered in memory of the dwarf scout's words, "Never knew no one who went in t'come back out."

Koun knows the way. He'll lead us to safety.

The course took a sudden turn and they filed carefully around the passage. Lia's heart thudded. The path narrowed, the ceiling lowered, and just as a twinge of panic took hold, a beam of light shot toward them. Lia caught a whiff of fresh air and fallen leaves.

We're almost there . . .

They hurried their pace, the horses bowing through the shrunken tunnel, and one by one, they burst through an opening into the heart of a familiar grove.

"The Bryns!" Wynn whooped.

Lia raised her face to the dusky sunlight. The foothills breathed renewed life into her. She turned back to the hollowed yew with her enhanced sight. Her hide-a-way shone back at her with reds and browns like polished jasper. A subtle glow emanated around the tree. She and Koun had spent many afternoons in the hollow's warm embrace, she never knowing it was a passage to Brume.

Lia peeked back inside the tree and found the tunnel gone. The hollow was just a hollow once more. However, she suspected the portal would open if ever the need arose.

She cast her gaze across the yellowing maple trees, her new eyes drinking in their brilliance. The familiar maples reached out like old friends. Their vibrant essence infused her with childhood memories and she reeled with longing. "Welcome home," they imparted.

The trees' greetings hushed under the pounding of hoof beats. A flash of black whipped through the trees. Wynn stepped forth and raised his blade. The ebony horse charged straight at them and Lia's stomach reached into her throat.

"Whoa!" Kelven halted his steed. "Wynn?"

He jumped down with his mouth agape. Wynn smiled, sheathed his sword, and clasped Kelven's arm. "You're in for a long story."

With his mouth still open, Kelven's eyes lit on Lia. His shock heralded her strange appearance. He drew close and pools of hazel-brown warmed her insides. "Are you . . . all right?"

She nodded, her throat dry as tinder. His eyes flickered over her face, up to her silver crown, and down to the tips of her moon-white fingers. He took her hand and held it like a flower, gentle and reverent, and then he pulled her into his arms. Lia melded her body into his, reveling in his warmth and tenderness. When he released her, his eyes were wet.

"I wondered why Koun kept leading me to the Bryns. For two days, the hound never let up on me. Now I know why." Kelven swallowed hard. "Listen, you both should know, your granda—"

"We know, Kel," Wynn said, sparing him from saying any more. "What of Lia's da; is there still time?"

Lia's insides froze. *Oh please . . .*

"He's alive," Kelven said, squeezing Lia's hand.

Without further delay, the trio sped the horses through the grove with Koun running alongside them. They reached the base of the hills edging Rockberg, and a gasp slid from Lia's lips.

Straif roots covered the ravaged village. The lifeless shoots dangled like webs from the rooftops and covered the ground in decaying heaps. A few cottages sent up wisps of hearth smoke, the only signs of life.

"Many fled, others died, and a few struggle to live." Kelven's voice cracked. "Koun and I have been hunting in the groves, and Doc Lloyd's been running up food and supplies from Kilnsgate. Last word he brought us was that the royals had arrived from Anu, making up their own explanation for this blight."

Kelven's words fell like whispers around Lia. "Da," was all she could say, all she could think about, as she hastened Merrie's step. Tears stung her eyes as they skirted the town. The hills rolled beside them with the quartz towers pointing at the twilight sky. They trampled over mounds of *Straif* roots, crushing the black arms to powder, and reached the edge of Lia's yard. An array of barbed shoots lay in tangles on the path, though none had made it to the cottage. They halted the horses and Lia hurried inside her home.

"Lia!" Ma's eyes turned to platters. She flew to her daughter and embraced her. They shared a flood of tears before Ma finally let go. She smoothed her hand over Lia's hair and ran her fingers down her cheek. "My starry heavens, what's happened to you?"

"I've been painted by Brume," Lia said. "But I'm alive."

Their tears did not cease as Ma embraced Wynn and Lia approached Da. She clasped his hand, still covered in green sores.

"He cannot wake. Most plagued by the poison have perished, but some, like your da, remain in this impervious sleep. That ointment you gave me before you left works like nothing else; not even the herbs Kelven brought from Brume measure as strong. It's the only thing that's kept his wounds from worsening."

Lia paused in memory. She reached for her pouch and the stone within grew hot. "The quartz dropped into the salve while I was filling the jar."

She eyed Ma. "I've much to tell you, but first we must craft the cure. I'll need you to come with me; you're part of the elixir."

"The what? Lia, shouldn't you rest for a moment? You and Wynn have wounds need tending—"

"No, we cannot delay." The silver waters lingered in her blood,

240

allaying the *Straif* venom's hold, but time ticked away its power, and only a few skins remained of the precious liquid. If she fell to the poison, so would the hope of the elixir.

"We'll be back," Lia said, nodding to Wynn and Kelven, and she and Ma hurried out the cottage door. She grabbed Merrie's reins, but stopped short when Ma waved her toward Da's workshop.

Lia rushed after her. "Ma, we must get to town, to the store—"

Her words froze as she charged into the room. Dozens of herb bundles dangled from the walls, mortars filled with crushed plants covered the largest table, and on a bench stood rows of jars filled with decoctions. Grandma's *Grimoire* lay open on its own table.

"You've done all this?" Lia said.

"No, not I, your cousin, Holly. She's here tending to the sick. She and your Aunt Brina should be arriving back soon." Ma's eyes welled up. "Holly sees things, has visions. She saw Granda's death, knew he perished after the journey home. So, they came here."

Lia held back her grief and whispered, "His spirit soars free in the Summerlands."

In their silence that followed, Lia's eyes roved to the opened *Grimoire*. One page showed the sketch of a tall fir and on the other page a flowery broom tree. Yet, that was not what pulled Lia closer to the book.

She blinked her eyes several times, but nothing changed. Her enchanted sight unveiled encryptions written on the pages she had never seen before. The writings blazed like wildfire across the finely sketched trees.

Upon the fir: *Accio donum vitae, beatus matrix,* and below it, the translation: "Summon gift of life, blissful womb." Across the broom tree were the words: *Devoco violentus ventus,* and below it: "Call away violent winds."

Lia flipped through the book, seeing for the first time the old widows' magic inscribed over the trees. So many chants, so many precious incantations Grandma cleverly hid. But now Lia had the sight to find them.

"What is it?" Ma asked.

Lia closed the book and turned to her. "It's time to purge the fog from everyone's eyes. No laws or foolish rules can deny the truths of magic. It runs through us all, and only when we turn our backs, when we shun the powers of nature, do we become prey to the darkness."

"You speak like a sage." Ma shook her head and sighed. "Your grandma used magic, upheld its powers in all sorts of ways, and yet she perished."

"Grandma Myrna danced with the shadows to get into Brume, bringing back curatives to all she could. She used her gifts the only way she knew how, from the place that breathed magic into her soul from her very beginning."

Ma's brow crinkled and she wrung her hands. Lia's heart ached for her. If only she had a balm to soothe Ma's grief over the loss of her parents.

They gathered supplies and toted them to the crystal tower at the center of Lia's garden. Soon, a cauldron dangled over a small fire, which sent flames to dance across the great quartz.

"So now it begins." Lia clasped Ma's hand under the starlit sky.

The words of the *Nion* guardian whispered across Lia's mind, and she recited them, "With three parts herbs we begin our cast, by lion's tooth and grass of goose, and slender shoots of quitch grass." She placed the cuttings from the three plants into the cauldron.

"And now we offer two parts tree, enchanted *Nion* and honey-sweet *Saille*." Lia placed the *Nion* clipping into the pot, and then uncoiled the *Saille* branch and placed it in, too.

"Add a snippet of golden bough, and bit of the enemy." Lia tossed in the golden bough found high in the *Duir* tree, and her heart warmed for Gobann, Laguz, and Othila. Then she withdrew the *Straif* piece. Ma sucked in her breath, but didn't speak. Lia let the piece roll in her palm, stiff and harmless. *Farewell, Hag-Mother.* And she dropped it into the pot.

Lia drew up a pouch and handed it to Ma, prompting her with a nod. Ma's hands trembled and her breath came heavy as she loosened the string and poured the glitter from its vessel.

"Combine with sacred alicorn," Lia said, as the sparkling essence from the unicorn's horn settled into the brew, "under the light of a sentry stone."

She released her crystal talisman from its pouch and it burned against her palm. Then a beam of light shot forth. Lia flinched, but held her stone steady. The crystal's mother—the tower before them—glowed in answer. Light formed at its center, expanding out until its entire mass radiated against the night. Lia's eyes widened on the giant quartz.

"Now, the water skin," she whispered, holding to the crystal's magic.

"Yes." Ma stammered. She grasped the skin and emptied the waters from the Seren River into the cauldron. "Ohhh."

"Brewed in the blood of Brume," Lia continued, "by maiden, mother, and crone."

"Mother!" Ma's face blanched nearly as white as Lia's.

Grandma Myrna hovered above, swathed in light. Her face emitted joy as she smiled on them. The cauldron steamed below her, the enchanted brew completed.

Lia's stone and the crystal tower dimmed. Grandma Myrna's spirit brushed across Lia's face like a feather. She floated before Ma and wrapped her ghostly arms around her daughter. Ma wept as if she'd tapped a spring. The elder woman glided upward and placed her hands on her heart. Ma and Lia mimicked the pose. "I love you too, Grandma," Lia said.

Grandma's soul sailed like a shooting star across the sky to paradise.

With blurred eyes and trembling hands, Lia filled several bottles with the elixir. Ma's sobs carried across the garden and Koun whimpered in reply. It had been less than a fortnight since Da's attack, but a lifetime of changes. More truths had been unveiled than Lia could have ever dreamed. Now, she held the cure to Draugyrd's bane in her hands. And creating it helped heal Ma's inner wounds, too.

Lia stumbled alongside Ma as they made it back into the cottage. She handed Kelven all but one of the bottles. "Give some to both horses, and then get to the others in town. One spoonful to each person should do."

With a nod, Kelven bolted from the cottage, and Lia turned to Da. Wynn sat near, his eyes heavy.

"Here, let me." Ma took the bottle and poured out a dose of the glittery substance.

Lia propped up Da's head and Ma spooned the magic in. He swallowed it in reflex.

"Wynn's turn, and then mine," Lia said.

Shock pinched Ma's forehead. "You and Wynn, too?"

She placed the bottle in Wynn's hand and he took a swig, and then handed it to Lia.

The warm liquid ran thick like honey down Lia's throat. She closed her eyes and swam in the euphoric magic. Her body warmed and her pains dissipated.

Ma's eyes rounded. "Look!"

Da grumbled and his head rolled on the pillow. His sores shrunk to pale green speckles and the swelling vanished. He moved his lips and his eyelids fluttered open upon Ma. "Carin."

Then his eyes shifted to Lia. "Daughter . . . what in tarnished augers . . . did you do to your hair?"

Family Tree

*L*ia awoke to the smell of porridge and honey biscuits, and a wet muzzle pressed against her face. "Guess you've had your morning milk." Koun licked his nose as Lia crawled out of bed.

Wynn's snoring carried through the cottage like a bear rumbling in his winter den. Da slept too, his body cured but weakened from days of fever. Lia smiled.

Soon, he'll be hammering away in his workshop, crafting furniture once again from the overgrowth of maples.

The kettle steamed and Lia poured herself a cup of chicory tea. She whirled around at the sound of the cottage door. Ma, Kelven, Aunt Brina, and Holly filed inside. Kelven stepped close and Lia's stomach did a flip. Tiredness from riding the night away weighed down his eyes, but he gave her a bright smile.

"I see my son is still sleeping. Might blow off this roof if he keeps at it." Aunt Brina squeezed Lia in a bosomy hug. "Hmph, hair the color of polished silver and skin like an eggshell. And Wynn looks like he's been struck by a thunderbolt. You're skinny as a withy to boot."

She turned and ladled a mound of porridge into a bowl and set it in front of Lia.

"Thanks, Aunt Brina. Good to see you too." Lia grinned at her aunt.

"You kids fill those scrawny bellies; you've all done a lifetime's work. Carin, my dear sister, your lover's fast asleep and there's a passel of apples begging to be picked." Aunt Brina shuffled herself back outside with Ma behind her.

Kelven swiped a biscuit from the platter and sat down across from Lia. He rubbed his eyes with a calloused knuckle. Holly sat beside him with a pouch strung around her neck.

"I'm glad you're back, Lia," she said. "I wasn't sure if, well, I didn't know if you'd make it after my vision."

"What did you see, cousin?" Lia spooned some porridge into her mouth.

"I was sitting in your garden, harvesting lemon balm when all at once I saw you cross to the Otherworld. And you, um, turned into a . . . tree."

Lia's eyes flitted to Kelven and then back to her eleven-year-old cousin. "I did cross over, Holly; your vision was right. But only for a moment, just a glimpse, and then I came back, pale as a birch."

Lia gulped some tea. "The tree you saw must've been the *Ruis* that I crossed over with; perhaps your vision muddled us together."

Holly didn't reply, but her eyes argued the point.

Lia pinched her lips. *A simple mix up, that's all it was.* Holly is new at scrying; she must've got confused with my connection to the *Ruis*. "So, what have you got in that pouch?"

"Oh, uh," Holly opened the small leather bag and released Grandma's amber into her palm, "Kelven let me hold it. When I first touched the amber, my mind filled with the sea—waves crashing on a hidden shore. Then I saw mountains, fog, and then a darkness. I was a little shaken afterward, but Kelven explained how the amber worked."

Lia gagged on her tea. "Holly, listen to me. Keep the stone in memory of Granda Luis and Grandma before him, but never think of wielding it to gain passage into Brume. All deals are off with the shades. You'd be killed at once, or worse."

Holly's amber eyes shone with fear. "I'd—"

"She'd never get by me to do anything that foolish." Wynn planted himself with a thud next to Lia. He scooped up the remaining biscuits and shoved them into his mouth, washing them down with tea. "So, everyone cured?"

Kelven piped up, "We got the elixir across Rockberg and to Doc Lloyd. He sent riders to the other villages. I put the last of the bottles in your da's workshop, Lia, along with the pile of gifts."

Lia cocked her head. "Gifts?"

"From all the families you saved. You and Wynn might as well be royalty now."

Wynn let out a cough and kicked Lia's foot under the table. "Royalty?"

Kelven's eyes squinted at Wynn. "You've got something to share?"

Wynn subdued his grin. "Later. Go on with what you were saying."

Kelven hesitated, then shifted his eyes back to Lia. "The people want to help you get the store back in order."

"That would be wonderful." *And surprising.*

For her entire life, she and Granda had endured the people's disapproval. It had taken the *Straif's* destruction to turn them back to embracing the old ways. Her heart tugged for Granda. She wished he could be here. He'd have loved nothing more than to help cultivate the healing crafts back into the lands.

Lia turned teary eyes on Holly. "Guess I'll need a partner, someone who could stay with me awhile."

Her cousin's eyes widened and she nodded.

Lia finished her porridge and stepped outside in a blaze of sunshine. A sense of a new era permeated the air. Her garden buzzed with life, and the herbs and flowers sang to her in greeting. The colors of the plantlife shone like gemstones, and she caught the flashing lights of tiny fae. She smiled at her newfound vision.

The stone tower rose from the center of her garden like a sculpture of ice. She thought of the light it exuded from the night before, and wondered if the magic from her little stone had strengthened its crystal-mother. Somehow, she had to find a way to help empower the quartz sentries of Rockberg.

Or the fog will continue to weaken.

She placed her hand on its smooth surface. Her pouch grew hot against her chest, and she drew out the stone into her other palm. A flash of light shot from the miniature quartz, encircling Lia and the crystal tower within it.

A great rumbling followed, and the tower filled with orange-red heat, as if molten lava boiled up from the earth's core. Lia's body shook with its energy and she strained to hold onto its power. The tower radiated like a thousand suns, shooting rays far to the north, toward Brume's looming wall. The fog spilled into her mind, hungry and cold, grasping at the fiery threads of light. Wherever the crystal's heat met cold, the fog thickened into strong, renewed billows.

Yes, it's working; it's strengthening the magic . . .

The cords of power fell as Lia collapsed.

"Lia!" Kelven leapt close, cupped her torso in his arms, and lifted her head. The light faded and her stone cooled. "Are you all right?"

She gazed into his worried eyes. "It's too much. I can't restore the power on my own."

Kelven's brow creased and he shook his head. "How 'bout you tuck that stone of yours away for a while. Even great wizards need a couple days off."

Lia gave him a wry grin and propped herself up. There was time. She would learn how to rally the magic, find a way to build up enough power, and revive the crystals to re-enchant the fog.

Koun planted himself next to Kelven, begging for a pet. "You know, this is some hound you've got here. I don't know if your ma told you, but he saved me twice."

"How?" Lia asked, slipping her pouch back under her tunic.

"I got about halfway through that fog when the amber started to glow. I tossed out the food and ale just like your granda had done. That's when I lost sight of the trail, couldn't find it anywhere. The wind started picking up and I thought sure I'd be swallowed up for good. Then I heard barking, and I knew the only creature capable of that howlish banter was Koun."

Koun rolled his body on the ground, dusting his back in earth. A couple of fae flashed against him.

"That's not all. That night, he started acting panicked, pacing and carrying on. When I opened the cottage door, I followed him out to hundreds of snakes creeping up the path. I realized they weren't snakes, but enormous roots. Koun leapt at them, wove through them like a wild thread, until they were all tangled. He didn't stop until the next day when the roots stopped moving."

Lia reached over Kelven's lap and patted her hound. When she turned back, her face came within inches of Kelven's. His breath brushed across her cheek. He ran his hand over her short locks and whispered, "Like spun silk."

Lia's stomach buzzed. She opened her mouth to speak, but he wrapped his hands around her waist and kissed her.

"Might wanna come up for air now. Your ma's coming this way," Wynn drawled.

Lia bolted from Kelven's lap. He unfolded himself from the ground, murmuring, "Beautiful."

Lia's heart sang. She was thin, pale as goat's milk, and silver-crowned, and he thought her beautiful.

"All rested and fed, I see. Good. And my strapping son is up and about." Aunt Brina huffed up the path with a basketful of apples.

"Let me help with those." Lia reached for the basket. Her aunt smiled. "Thank you, dear one. You boys come inside with me. It's time for a nice long chat."

Kelven gave Lia a wink before he and Wynn followed Aunt Brina through the door.

"Been nice having my sister here, strongest woman I've ever known." Ma set her basket down and pushed wisps of copper hair back into her bun. "Lia, let's sit awhile."

They found a spot near Da's workshop, dotted with wildflowers. In the distance, Merrie and Nolan grazed peacefully alongside Lia's young bay, Shae.

Ma turned to her with a somber face. "I knew of the shades—

253

wind wraiths allowing Grandma to pass through the fog. She told me they let her in for the enchanted food and ale she brought them, but I knew there was a greater cost. I felt it in her desperation, watched her run like wildfire back and forth from Brume, crafting potions all hours, or writing in her *Grimoire*. There was never time for sleep, barely time for any of us. Every day she raced the same, as if each second bit at her heels like a beast. After she died, I vowed never to follow in her footsteps, never to give my life over that way."

Ma dabbed her eyes with her apron. "Then my worst nightmares happened. Oh, your granda assured me you'd all be safe, that he'd gone in numerous times without incident. Then Kelven brought back his poisoned body, told me you and Wynn had stayed in that wretched place, and the next day, my father died."

"I'm sorry, Ma. I miss Granda, too." Lia put her arm around her ma's shoulders. "It's over now, and in time the village will mend."

"Oh, how I wish it were over, but I knew it the minute I saw you. My sister knows it, too. You, Wynn, Kelven, even Holly, all of you carrying the burdens of Brume."

Lia paused, finding no words to ease Ma's fears. The strange land had gripped them all and changed their lives forever. The last line of the riddle trickled like rain through her mind:

I know the children will come forth and bring it back again.

Yes, she thought, *and we have only just begun.*

Their silence hung like the travel-worn clothes drying on the line. The ragged garments dangled in the breeze. "Sorry about your cloak, Ma; I know how you love it."

"The cloak was beautiful, but that's not why I love it," Ma said. "It carries something special. The soft inner lining is your swaddling blanket—the same blanket my mother used with me, from the same cloth used to swaddle her."

Lia bolted to the clothesline and released the tattered cloak. Her fingers trembled as she pulled at the seams, releasing the smooth lining from its woolen shell. She flipped it over to its other side and ran her hands over the green dyed velvet, worn and flat from time.

Ma rushed to her side. "What is it? What are you doing?"

Lia held up her birth blanket and her eyes fixed on the oversized patch adorning its upper corner. She grabbed hold of her knife and cut away the stitches. The flowery patch fell away. In its place, embroidered on blue velvet, stretched a long bow set with an arrow, entwined in ivy, and aimed toward the sky.

Ma's eyes widened. "But that's . . . it can't be." She ran her hand over the crest.

"It's the royal crest. This mantle belonged to Grandma's father, King Gorsedd."

Ma trembled and Lia's mind spun with a new horror. Remnants of the precious mantle lay strewn in Brume's *Eadha* forest, stained scarlet from her many wounds. On any other cloth, the magic of her blood would wither away. But on the mantle, her blood mingled with the imprints of birth blood from maiden, mother, and crone. The imprints would cradle her spilled essence—preserve it.

And give Draugyrd a way to bind me!

A telling verse from the *Grimoire* cut into her mind like an icy dagger:

> *Birth from blood, life's primal key,*
> *Vital force, sap from the tree;*
> *Flowing rivers, essence of you*
> *Spill gently forth your sacred brew.*

Vital force, essence of you. Blood was a sacred elixir all on its own, one to be cherished, revered, and rarely spilled. Lia knew a few concoctions that used it for the good, but most magic requiring blood was baneful and dark. Now her precious blood, her sacred brew, stained remnants of the royal cloth that lay strewn like treasures across Draugyrd's forest.

Her insides quivered with dread. She could almost hear the master shade's laughter. *How soon until Draugryd recovers from the battle? How long do I have before he works out the binding magic and pulls me back to his lair?*

Lia's mind flooded with the fateful whispers of the prophecy found deep within Granda's cane:

> *A child of imposing grace will shine for all the land;*
> *From moon to moon she will race, as armies take their stand.*
> *Across the kingdom her foe will chase,*
> *As her soul strives to stay free,*
> *And in the end her freedom resides*
> *Within the great hallowed tree.*

"Carin, Lia, come quick," Aunt Brina called.

A caravan meandered up the road in a blaze of color. Silken flags of reds and golds glimmered, all embroidered with the same royal crest gripped within Lia's hands. The band of Nemetona's soldiers rode in perfect unison, leading two fine carriages curtained in crimson.

Crimson. The color of the royal sages.

Acknowledgements

Thanks first and foremost to my husband and sons for supporting me through the long, roller-coaster process of writing a novel. I'd also like to thank my grandmother and late grandfather for their inspiration, my dad for cheering me on, my mom for her belief in me, my brother for being as fantasy-nerdy as I am, and all my relatives and friends who listened to me ramble about my book.

A big thanks goes out to my writing friends for their guidance and encouragement. I'm grateful and proud to rub elbows with such creative people. A special thanks to Susan Salluce for pushing me to get this book out to the world, and my heartfelt thanks to the ladies over at indie-visible.com for rallying their support and awing me with their talents.

About the Author

Christina Mercer earned a degree in Accounting from California State University at Sacramento and a Certificate in Herbal Studies from Clayton College of Natural Health. She took Writer's Best in Show at the 2012 SCBWI CA North/Central Regional Conference and was a semi-finalist in the 2010 Amazon Breakout Novel Award Contest. Christina resides in Northern California enjoying life with her husband, two sons, four dogs, three fish, and about 100,000 honeybees.

You can find her at www.christinamercer.com
or blogging with the girls over at www.indie-visible.com

CPSIA information can be obtained
at www.ICGtesting.com
Printed in the USA
LVOW11s0105021116
511203LV00002BA/136/P